Greylands

Isobelle Carmody was born in Wangaratta, Victoria, Australia. She writes science fiction, fantasy, children's and juvenile literature and divides her time between a home on the Great Ocean Road in Australia and her travels abroad.

Isobelle began work on the highly acclaimed *Obernewtyn Chronicles* when she was just fourteen years old. She continued to work on these while completing a Bachelor of Arts, and a cadetship in journalism. The first two books in the *Obernewtyn* series were short-listed for the CBC Children's Book of the Year in the Older Readers category; *Scatterlings* won Talking book of the Year. *The Gathering* was a joint winner of the 1993 CBC Book of the Year Award and the 1994 Children's Literature Peace Prize. *Greylands* won the 1997 Aurealis Award for Best Young Adult Novel and a White Raven at Bologna, while *Billy Thunder and the Night Gate* was short-listed for the Patricia Wrightson Prize for Children's Literature in the 2001 NSW Premier's Literary Awards. Both *Little Fur* and *A Fox Called Sorrow* received BAAFTA Industry Awards for design and *Alyzon Whitestarr* won the coveted Golden Aurealis for overall best novel at the Aurealis Awards. Her book for younger readers, *The Red Wind*, won the Children's Book Council Book of the Year in 2011.

Isobelle is currently working on the sequel to *The Red Wind*, *The Cloud Road*.

Also by Isobelle Carmody

The Obernewtyn Chronicles
Obernewtyn
The Farseekers
Ashling
The Keeping Place
The Stone Key
The Sending

The Legend of Little Fur Series
Little Fur
A Fox Called Sorrow
A Mystery of Wolves
A Riddle of Green

The Kingdom of the Lost
The Red Wind

Other Books
Alyzon Whitestarr
The Gathering
Green Monkey Dreams
Metro Winds

GREYLANDS

Isobelle Carmody

FORD ST

For Jan

Thanks to Heather Giles for reading and making corrections to the manuscript and a special thank you to Deb Gates for the final, vital read through of the revised version; in memory of her Lissa.

First published by Penguin Books Australia, 1997
This revised edition published 2012 by Ford Street Publishing,
an imprint of
Hybrid Publishers, PO Box 52, Ormond VIC 3204
Melbourne Victoria Australia

2 4 6 8 10 9 7 5 3 1

www.fordstreetpublishing.com

National Library of Australia Cataloguing-in-Publication data:
Carmody, Isobelle, 1958–
Greylands / Isobelle Carmody.

ISBN 9781921665677 (pbk.).

Cover design: © Grant Gittus

Printed in Singapore by KHL Printing Co Pte Ltd

Foreword

When I set out to write *Greylands*, I wanted to look at the surreal world you enter when you are in a state of grief, and I wanted to do that from the point of view of a child. I wanted to reflect the fact that the grief of a child is no less profound and deep and serious than the grief of an adult, but that it is experienced differently because children have a different knowledge of the world and live beneath the eye line of, and within a world created and controlled by, adults.

I chose this subject because I was (and am) haunted by the surreal world I entered when I was a child after my father died in a car accident – the feeling that the world had been wrenched out of joint and that nothing worked the way it had before. Connections were broken, links severed, and nothing would ever be the same again.

I remember vividly stepping out into the world the day after he died, distorted with the hugeness of my loss, seeing the sun shining, birds singing, people laughing and talking as if nothing had happened, laughter coming from the window of a passing car.

I was shocked by the discovery that the whole world was not grief-stricken and shattered, too. They did not even know that my father had died! It was one of those moments when you truly understand that you are separate from the world and from other people.

I recognised that the things my younger self had felt were deep and important and that they had affected her, altered her, and reshaped her. I recognised that this death and her grief had gone on affecting the child that grew into a woman and then into the woman I was, about to write *Greylands*; a woman who, to some extent, was still grieving for the father-hero who died so suddenly and tragically.

I wanted to explore that surreal, remembered world of child grief, because I wanted to see how it linked to my grief as an adult. I wanted to find out how exactly one negotiated that surreal, shifty, colourless land one is transported to, by grief. I wanted to find out if there was anything important or nourishing or beautiful to be discovered in that bleak terrain. I wanted to understand how one endures grief, and how one survives it. I wanted to understand what surviving it had done to me.

I don't know where Jack came from – he arrived unexpectedly, a tallish, slightly built boy of twelve. I did not consciously choose his sex. I have never consciously chosen the sex of a character in a story. Indeed they seem to spring fully fledged from my brow, and always with full personalities and partial histories, though their faces are often unclear to me. I think I craft them in my subconscious as vessels that will be the right shape to carry whatever questions are at the heart of the piece of writing they will inhabit. I don't write notes but I think long and hard about stories before I begin them, and that, I think, is when a character fulfills their secret gestation.

Were I to guess, I would say Jack is a boy for the same reason Nathaniel in *The Gathering* was a boy. I seem unable to allow my young female main characters to be anything but strong and rather driven, because that was what I felt I needed to be, to survive childhood. But I can permit a boy character a greater softness or vulnerability, because he is a step further from the child that I once was.

But that is just my guess, which is as good or bad as anyone else's. The truth is that I don't know.

Certainly I was taken aback at Jack's age. He was the youngest character that had ever stepped onto the stage of my imagination in a main role. I had always felt characters that were not at least in their teens would force me to limit my perceptions of the world and the events in the story, the words I would use to express them. But Jack arrived and I could no more send him back than send my newborn daughter back insisting that I wanted a boy.

I began to look at the world through Jack's eyes, and immediately recognised that children do not perceive less of the world than adults. It is only that they must express what they see differently, lacking adult tools. And surely, if I wanted to express the profound complexity of a child's grief I had to find a way to do that in a child's voice. I had to bridge the gaps in a child's knowledge of the world, as a child would do – with poetry and imagination.

Some of the gaps exist because of things a child has not yet been told or which it has understood incompletely or incorrectly. Other gaps exist because there are things they have not enough life experience to fully understand, or because someone chose to withhold some information from them.

This latter gap struck me as being vitally important to my story. So many times in workshops when students have been working on pieces about childhood, they recall not being told things, which they nevertheless intuited. Many of the events remembered concerned death – the death of an animal or a sibling or parent. Often it is the means of death that will be withheld, but somehow the child is aware of it, even in a distorted form. I knew that the ability of the child to absorb through its pores what had been withheld or concealed, must also be part of my story.

I was completely engaged and committed to my story now, and in love with the way the children in it turned complex thoughts and feelings and ideas into beautiful, broken, poetic language. In fact I loved it so much that I spontaneously bestowed a little sister on Jack, so I could further explore that poetic coding. Ellen, too, came fully formed, smart and wise and sweet. I adored her as did Jack so that she became the heart of his house and of my story.

I already knew that their mother had died. I had not figured out how. I thought maybe a tragic accident, but I didn't want to coldly decide. So, Jack would have some of the facts, but not all, and I would learn what happened as he figured it out. I know this sounds as if the death was a real event that I was researching, but often writing does feel as if you are discovering something that already exists. Maybe that is because a lot of it is built in and of your subconscious.

I knew, in the same way that I knew the mother had died tragically, that the father was shattered and withdrawn. His emotional state was vital to the story because the grief of the adults around the child had to be taken into account. Don't children grow up in a world created by the adults who are their carers, after all? Not just the physical world that is of their making and choosing and buying, but also an emotional world made up of their fears and angers, triumphs and disappointments. Wasn't that how it had been when my father died? Hadn't I had to negotiate my mother's grief, her fears, and her feelings of helplessness?

So Jack's sorrow at his mother's death and his natural drive to understand what happened, must take place within the world of his father's grieving. Hence Jack finds himself drawn again and again into the colourless, silent, tasteless greylands, where he must discover the truth about his mother's death if he is to save himself and his father, and return home to Ellen.

I began to write, and as always when a piece of writing is taking me deep, there is a powerful current that begins to drag in the real world.

As it happened, I was living in Prague at the time and looking back, I am astounded at how much of my daily life was absorbed by the story. For instance, I was often struck by how closed and hard people's expressions were. Like clenched fists. I understood this to be the result of the political oppressions they had endured, but it struck me it was also an expression of a strangely aimless grief, not at a death but at the strangling of spirit and soul that was life under the lid of communism. I thought how countries could also be grief-stricken; that it might be as difficult for them to recover as for an individual. So the idea of a place where grief oppresses all who live there crept into the mix.

Even the title to the book comes from a journey I tried to make from Tallinn in Estonia, overland to Paris via Prague, on a Eurorail pass. I had a map issued by Eurorail, which showed Europe, but a large portion was grey instead of coloured. After I was thrown off at a border at 3 am one morning because I required a visa that I didn't have, it came to me that the grey land on the map was a territory where things – tickets, feelings, and relationships – did not work as they were expected to do. Those who travelled there had come to a place exempt from the rules of normality.

I did not plan these aspects of the book.

But ultimately writing is a journey into mystery, and no amount of clever planning before or cunning decoding afterwards, will clear away all the mist of the deepest tales.

Don't get me wrong. Writing is a craft and mostly I feel very engaged and focused and intent and practical when I am doing it. I am not smoking and drinking and being bohemian. I am not waiting for a muse to come flapping down. But there is always the hope that the X factor will arise and turn a carefully planned story into something that cuts very deep. This is more likely to happen when you are in the habit of drawing on your own life experience to write, when you delve into events that intrigue or frighten or trouble you than if you are the sort of writer who doggishly plots a story to catch the latest fashion train rushing by on its way to oblivion.

There is an ancient alchemy between the writer and their idea, and if the writer is really lucky, some other factor will emerge, which might just as well be called factor X.

This unknown ingredient is most often randomly

supplied by life. It might be an incident glimpsed from the bus window on the way to the swimming pool, an interview heard on the car radio, a snatch of song, a conversation between two children about the meaning of a story in a book, a laugh or a cry. Or it might be the sight of a grey tower through the mist at a train station in the lightless early hours of a freezing winter day. It might be the colours of a map, the memory of a funeral and a mother, weeping uncontrollably, the sound of a dog barking or a burst of rich, compelling laughter.

Whatever it is, it will crack you and the story wide open and suddenly you are in freefall, going deeper than you imagined.

Naturally, there is a risk involved. You might find yourself confronting something with sharp teeth or a savage sting. You might even be devoured. For once you leave the carefully plotted path, there is no telling what you will discover or where you will end up. This is where writing requires courage; a readiness to venture into the dark, a willingness to incise painful wounds, to lance infected swellings, to probe the shadows and to look under the bed where the id and the ego lurk.

But while stories that carry a writer into uncharted territory may indeed lead them to places where there are dragons waiting to devour them, or worse, to nothing at all, there is a tremendous sense of freedom in such journeying. And there may be wonders to discover, if you can endure the terror that you have gone too far and might never find your way back, that you will be devoured or that your journey may be fruitless.

If you do write such a story, and end up making such a perilous journey; if you do not turn back or baulk at what you find, you may well return with a tale that has something true and potent at the heart of it.

Greylands was such a journey for me, and I am profoundly happy to have it in print again. Because that grief-stricken girl whose father died is me, and I am still being changed by what happened to her all those years ago. For we do not lose or discard the child inside ourselves when we become adults. We are all the ages we have ever been, each age cupped inside the next, like a thousand matryoshka dolls.

Journey with me now through the mirrors into the greylands . . .

Isobelle Carmody
Melbourne 2012

The Beginning

'That's not the beginning,' Ellen said, pointing to where Jack had written about the sky.

'Stop reading over my shoulder,' he ordered.

'But you said you were writing about how it was after Mama died.'

'I am, but I'm telling it my way.'

'What does that mean? You're making stuff up?'

Jack thought about it. 'You have to. Real life isn't like a story with a beginning and a middle and an end. It's everybody's stories all muddled together. But this will be my story and I'm starting with me dreaming that Mama told me she had wings.'

'She did tell us she had wings,' Ellen said.

'I know she did. That's why I put it in.'

Ellen said, 'I think you should start: Once upon a time, in a faraway land, Jack had a dream. Like that.'

'Well, it's my story and it didn't happen in a faraway land . . .'

'If it's not going to be facts, you can make the story happen anywhere you like,' Ellen said.

Jack frowned. 'That's true . . .'

Chapter 1

Jack dreamed of his mother.

In the dream, they were walking along a beach together. The sky was the colour of fogged metal and the sea was grey except for one bright patch covered with sequins of light.

'Look!' His mother pointed to the clouds all piled up and squashed together along the horizon. 'See that city in the sky? There's the castle and there's the street leading down to the town, and there's a river right through the middle . . .'

Jack nodded, though he couldn't quite see those things.

'I came from the clouds,' she whispered into his ear. 'I fell to earth, but that's where I started out. I married your father because he said he couldn't live without me and he wouldn't mind if I sometimes longed for the sky.'

Jack made his face into a mask, keeping his thoughts hidden behind it. His mother liked to tell them weird things, and later laugh and admit she had made them up. Stringing them along like that.

But lately she was just as likely to mean whatever strange things she said, and it was safer not to react until you were sure.

'You can only get there if you can fly,' his mother said softly. She tapped her shoulders. 'I have wings, but you can't see them. I will carry you with me . . .' She reached for Jack, her eyes gleaming and feral.

Jack woke, his heart banging at his ribs. The dream had seemed so real that he felt he could still hear the high, wild sound of her laughter, and smell the sweet, peppery scent she had liked.

'Dead,' he said aloud, and the word sounded like a door slamming in an empty house. He tried again. 'She's dead.' Now it sounded flat and fake, like the noise of a real gun after you get used to the movie sound of one. Or real punches when you were expecting Batman *ka-pows*. The word 'dead' never sounded right on his lips, but maybe that was because of thinking all the time about his mother being dead. Like looking at a word so much that it stops meaning anything.

Or maybe 'dead' was just a word that would always sound wrong.

He stretched, and some cold slithered in under the blankets to snuggle up beside him. He lay still until it melted away.

He had been waking up in the night a lot lately. He would dream that he was walking, and then the sound of laughter would wake him. Or he would dream of his mother and the dream would turn into a nightmare, like tonight. Sometimes he woke only an hour after he had gone to bed, and then the whole night would stretch out to be endured.

It was so hard to go back to sleep once you came awake, Jack thought. Your eyes stared into the shadows, trying to see if anything was there; your ears strained to hear; and the night was full of movements.

He sat up finally, thirsty and needing to go to the toilet. He had been feeling he had to go for a while, but he had hoped the urge would disappear so that he would not have to get out of bed. He knew there was nothing looking at him out of the half-opened wardrobe, of course, and no drooling thing under his bed waiting to grab his bare ankle, and nothing lurking in the hallway. But still, it was a creepy business being up in the night when everyone else was in bed. The house seemed to change shape so that there were more corners with shadows thick in them, like leaves blown up against a grate.

But need was need and he was suddenly desperate. He swung his feet out of the warm blankets and onto the wooden floor.

It felt cold but he hurried across to the door, his hand groping for the switch. Light filled the room, banishing the slysome shadows that distorted everything and rustled like clothes swishing on the floor, or creaked like boards when you trod on them.

Idiot, Jack jeered at himself. After all, if there was a six-foot hairy fanged monster in the room, what would the light do? Stab its eyes out? Just the same, the light made him feel better.

It was funny how night seemed to make him a different shape, too, like it did with the house. He became smaller and younger and more nervous. A baby deer: all ears and eyes, his legs tremblingly ready to carry him away from danger.

He opened his bedroom door and reached his hand around to switch on the hall light. He always did this – making a path of light through the dark-ness. The toilet was through the kitchen at the end of the hall, and he wished yet again that they were rich enough to have a toilet and bathroom leading right from his room like his friend Mario did.

Passing his sister's bedroom, he glanced in.

Light fell on Ellen in a broad bright slice, but she was not disturbed by it because her face was half pushed into the pillow. She always burrowed into sleep like a little animal going into its lair. He was tempted to go over and give her a cuddle. She didn't act like the sisters of his friends, showing off and screaming. She could really sit still and when she did talk, it would be to ask some odd question no one else would ever have thought of, or to tell you something she had figured out.

One time their mother had been straining the pips from some freshly squeezed orange juice and

Ellen asked why she did that. She had been at the age when she asked why about everything and came back with another why when you answered her and another why after that.

Instead of saying it made the juice bitter, their mother said that trees grew from seeds and, if you swallowed them, eventually a forest would grow inside you. Ellen had liked the idea of that, but their mother said ominously that a whole forest wouldn't fit inside a person.

A few days later, Jack caught Ellen putting a seed into her mouth.

'I'm big enough for one little tree, aren't I?' she asked earnestly.

'One little tree would be fine,' Jack assured her, hiding his smile. After that he often asked her how the tree was and she would always say she could feel it growing. Sometimes she said the roots were stretched into her feet and they made her want to walk barefoot in the dirt, and other times she would sigh and say all those branches and leaves in her brain were tangling up her thoughts and making her tired, or she would say the wind was inside her, whispering in the branches.

It got so that Jack could actually imagine that tree growing with Ellen year after year. He even felt that was why she was so hungry to know things all the time. She was feeding her tree.

'What kind of tree?' Mario asked her; when she

agreed that he could be let in on the secret.

'The tree of knowledge,' she said. Which wiped the grins off their faces, because if you were going to grow a tree inside of you, what other tree would you want but the tree of knowledge?

Mario liked Ellen and he never wanted her to go away and leave them alone when he visited. He was always asking her things to see what she would answer. He said she cracked him up.

Of course, Mario didn't come around to their place any more. Jack had stopped asking him because a visit would mean Mario would see the great, gaping hole his mother's death had left in their lives, and Jack would have to see it all over again through his friend's eyes.

Staring at Ellen now, Jack found himself wishing that she would wake up, but she wouldn't unless he shook her.

She sleeps like the dead, his mother always said.

Jack shivered and went on down the hall.

He came to his parents' door, which was slightly ajar, and he could not resist putting his head in. For a split second the longing to find everything as it had been was so strong that he actually saw her there, the dark hair splayed on her pillow, half veiling her white face.

But it was just his father, curled on the side of the bed where his mother had once slept. One hand gripped the pillow, and he was frowning in his sleep.

He muttered something, and clawed at his chest before becoming still again.

Jack's father was a tall man with big hands and broad shoulders and curling hair the colour of the bitter, dark chocolate his mother had liked. He never shouted, and when he smiled you could hear the warmth of it in his voice. His eyes were watchful, though. Mario said that was probably on account of him being a policeman. But Ellen had eyes like that too, so maybe it was hereditary.

Asleep, his father looked small, Jack reflected, and then felt guilty for the thought, which seemed to be a betrayal of them both. It forced him to acknowledge that his father had shrunk since the death of his wife and maybe that was something Jack didn't want to see. Like his father crying so hard at the funeral that people stared at them all.

His mother had taught them that looking was fine, but staring was bad manners. Sometimes she made faces if she caught them looking at her for too long, because then, she said, it turned into staring. Some of her faces were really funny and Jack would nearly choke laughing if they were eating. Others were kind of horrible, but that was what came from having a mother who was an actress before she started being a mother. Sometimes she was too good at pretending.

Jack went the rest of the way down the corridor

and through the kitchen to the toilet, switching on lights as he went.

It was freezing on the tiles and he pulled his pyjamas down and stood on them. His pee trickled loudly into the toilet bowl and he remembered how he used to believe that there was something inside it when he was little. Something like a banksia man with vampire fangs.

He had told his mother, hoping she would laugh, because her laughter was like switching on a light. But she laughed less and less over the years, and that time she had looked very serious and told him there were lots of places in the world where bad things hid themselves.

'Cracks especially. You have to be careful of the cracks. Sometimes they are disguised as something else. A doorway, or a smile or even a winking eye. And if you fall through them, you never know where you will end up.'

That scared Ellen, but as usual in those days, Jack hadn't known whether their mother was joking or serious, and so he had smiled tentatively, ready to withdraw it quickly if that proved to be the wrong reaction.

Once, not long before she died, he had laughed at something he thought was a joke, and she had shaken him so hard his teeth rattled. Actresses were highly strung. That's what his father said to people whenever his mother went off the deep end. It seemed to Jack, thinking back, that she had became more and more moody. If television channels were emotions you could tune into, she had become a channel surfer.

A memory came to him of her slapping Ellen's cheek so hard that it left a red handprint. It was as if a string snapped in her then. Ellen had not cried, but his mother had. She had sobbed and sobbed, and Ellen had patted her dark hair, saying it didn't matter, that everything was all right. Just for a second, it was like his little sister was the mother.

That happened the same week their mother had died. She had been so strange and tense by then that anything would make her angry or upset.

It was Mario's theory that you knew you were going to die right before the end — not in the front of your mind where it would block out everything else, but right deep in the back, so you could sort of get prepared without even knowing it.

'Remember how weird Tornado was the morning before she got hit by a car?' he had insisted.

Tornado had been one of Mario's pet mice, and she *had* acted weird that day, running frantically around on her wheel, which she did a lot, then leaping wildly off the top, which she had never done before. Later in the day, she escaped while Mario was cleaning the cage. She raced across the lawn, through the fence, over the footpath and onto the road. A car had run over her and the poor lady driving felt so bad because there was nothing left but a disgusting wet blotch on the road.

'Tornado was sick, I reckon, or she wouldn't have run away like that,' Jack had told Mario.

'She acted weird *because* she felt sick, not because she knew she was going to get squashed and dead. Maybe you would know you were going to die if it was a heart attack or something like that. Your body would know in advance because things would be happening inside it. But how could you know you were going to die in a car accident? That would be like seeing into the future.'

That started Mario off on his favourite subject: the psychic abilities of animals. Actually, that was his second favourite topic. The first was *animals* full stop. Which was probably why he planned on being a vet when he grew up, even though it took about a million years of going to school.

'Vets have to be detectives because animals don't show they're in pain,' Mario said reverently. 'They *endure.*'

Of all the things he loved about animals, it was their ability to bear things – to endure – that Mario admired most.

That was something Jack's mother and Mario had in common: their love of animals. It was this that had brought Mario into their lives. He had knocked on the door, a scruffy, dark-haired, dark-eyed kid with a chip in his front tooth and a limp cat in his arms. Jack's mother had gasped and ushered him in, and they started examining the cat right there on the hall table.

Jack's mother had run her fingers over it and said she thought it was shocked though otherwise unhurt, but you never knew and so they would take it to the vet.

It wasn't until they were all waiting at the vet's – Ellen and Jack and their mother and their old retriever, Lily, who was so senile by then she probably thought they were there for her, and Mario, whose name they still didn't know – that it came out the cat wasn't Mario's. He had found it outside their house and assumed it was theirs because of the way Jack's mother had reacted. She, of course, assumed it was Mario's because who else would pick up a dead-looking cat but its grief-stricken owner? Neither of them had recognised in the other a true animal lover until that moment in the vet's waiting room.

By then the cat had recovered from its dopiness and started yowling in protest at being catnapped by a bunch of strangers. Nevertheless, Jack's mother insisted on it being given a clean bill of health by the vet before they took him back and released him.

It was so late by then that Mario ended up staying for dinner. That was when they learned he was new to the neighbourhood and would be going to the same school as Jack and Ellen. Some time later, Mario told them his parents had split up and he had chosen to stay with his father, rather than go with his mother and her boyfriend to the city. He told Jack he just couldn't bear to leave his father all alone.

As a family they all seemed pretty cool about the split, which meant Mario had two nice homes and two sets of birthday and Christmas presents. 'They still love *me*,' he told Jack once.

Jack remembered thinking he would rather get one set of presents from one set of parents who loved each other. But that was before, when he had two parents instead of a dead mother and a father who had turned into one of the living dead.

Now he wished with all his heart that his mother lived in the city with a boyfriend so he could visit her in the holidays and every other weekend.

When school started after Christmas, Jack and Mario ended up in the same class and that sealed their friendship. They were like Laurel and Hardy, or Abbott and Costello. Or *not* like them, Jack's father had said in his dry, funny way, since those guys had hated one another.

He had been like that back then, Jack's father. Always coming out with unusual bits of information. He had noticed everything. Mario said it was the way a policeman's mind worked. They stored things for future reference: faces, streets, crime scenes. Mario believed that Jack's father would be so polite and gentle with crooks that they would think him gormless and let their guard down. All the time his eyes would be taking everything in, sifting it and building an airtight case. Certainly there was very little Jack's father didn't see, and though his mother used to joke that it was like living with the thought police, it had always made Jack feel safe to have his father watching over them all like that. Nothing bad could happen, you felt, under that gaze.

But of course, something bad had happened. Something worse than bad. Maybe that was why his father no longer had that watchful look. Maybe because all the watchfulness in the world had not kept his wife safe.

Soberly, Jack flushed the toilet, pulled up his pyjamas and went into the bathroom to wash his hands. It was all shiny black tiles. He didn't like it much because those tiles were too much like black mirrors. He had disliked mirrors ever since he'd seen a pantomime when he was little about the wicked queen in Snow White. 'Mirror, Mirror on the wall,' the wicked queen had chanted, and then her mirror, or something inside it, answered in a snaky slithering voice. There had been a sort of face in the mirror, and it had scared him so badly he'd peed himself a little bit, but not enough for anyone to notice.

'Never trust a mirror,' his mother had told him. 'They never tell the truth unless you make them.'

'You'll fill his head with nonsense,' his father said, smiling and shaking her a little. 'He has to understand that some things are real and others, not. Children need things defined.'

Defined was a word like knife, Jack thought. It was like something that cut. A broken mirror could cut you worse than any knife. Mario had an uncle who had cut his hand on a mirror. It got infected and his hand blew up and turned green, and they had to chop it off. Fingering the puckered pink lump at the end of his arm, he had told Jack that he could *feel* the hand sometimes, like its ghost was still there.

Jack turned on the tap over the gleaming basin and washed his hands, then leaned over and had a long slurping drink.

As he straightened, without meaning to, he met his own eyes in the mirror. That made his heart jump hard against his chest. Bang! Like someone had given him a punch. He stepped back quickly. The boy in the mirror withdrew, too, but they could not unlock their eyes. Jack began to feel he couldn't breathe properly because, although it was only himself he was looking at, it seemed like it was *not* him as well.

'You can't fool me,' he said softly. The boy in the mirror mouthed the same words, then smiled mockingly as if to say: your move.

'The queen protects the king,' Jack whispered, the words coming from somewhere inside him. His mother had taught him how to play chess and he always thought of her as the queen. The most important piece in the game, she could go anywhere and do almost anything any other piece could do. The week his mother died, they had played, but she had lost her queen. You always knew it was pretty much over after that. She had tipped over her king in surrender, giving Jack a quick, angry look.

It was creepy how clearly he could remember things about that last week.

The chess game and Ellen cutting her finger and their father saying he was to be promoted again. He even remembered the man who came to the door and sold their mother a set of encyclopaedias on trial. 'You can send them back if you're not satisfied one hunnert per cent,' the man had promised, smiling a big, white, advertising smile, slurring his words with the excitement of a sale. Jack even remembered that the salesman's name was Dabney Gate, and that he wore a gold pinkie ring.

The more he thought about it, the more Jack remembered. The wattle-pattern dress his mother wore the day before she died, the red dress Ellen wore the day their mother died, the peculiar look on their mother's face when she said, 'Let's go to the fun park. We'll be children together.'

The mirror rippled.

Jack's mouth fell open and his heart tried hard to climb out of it. He clenched his teeth and strove to drag his gaze sideways. It was no good. His eyes were riveted to the mirror. He began to panic.

The mirror rippled harder, as if it was water

and someone was blowing on it, and Jack could no longer see his face. He could still see his eyes, but all around them the pink of his flesh swam and blurred. He opened his mouth to cry out, but all at once the mirror began to settle. When it was perfectly still, the face looking into Jack's was not his own! He was looking at a pretty girl with dark shining eyes and crow-black hair framing a white face.

Jack swayed forward, really feeling he might faint. He reached out to steady himself, touching the mirror.

Chapter 2

Jack opened his eyes. He was lying on his back staring at a white light hanging from a white roof.

'Hello,' said a girl, leaning over him and smiling upside-down.

Jack blinked up at her. Though she was a stranger, her dark, swinging hair and pale, heart-shaped face were familiar.

'Sit up, why don't you?' she suggested. 'The dizziness comes when you cross, but it gets better once you start moving.'

Jack did not answer her. He was staring at her rudely because she was absolutely colourless. Her eyes and hair were black, her skin and teeth white, her lips grey, exactly the same ambiguous grey as the sky outside the frosted bathroom window.

Grey? But it had been night . . .

Jack noticed a huge lump on the girl's back under her cloak. He forced himself not to stare at it as he stood up. It must be bad to be both an albino and have a hump. 'Who are you?' he asked.

She bent down to scoop up a cloth bundle from

the floor. 'I have to go. They can tell when someone crosses and they'll be here any minute.'

'What are you talking about?' Jack demanded, struggling to his feet. 'Who are you and what are you doing in my house?'

'It's not your house,' she said, going out of the bathroom.

'I suppose it's yours . . .' He had followed her, but his protests died in his mouth, because instead of coming into the blue kitchen, they entered a dove-grey hall which led to a front door he had never seen before in his life.

He was in someone else's house!

Horrified, he decided he must have slipped and hit his head in the bathroom, then had somehow wandered outside and into this girl's house. 'I guess I banged my head,' he told himself.

The girl nodded. 'No one can come here unless they are wounded.' Before Jack could ask what she meant, she said, 'The longer you're here the harder it is to go back.'

'Back where?' he asked cautiously.

'Back through the mirror, stupid.'

'Through the mirror . . .' Jack echoed, but surprise melted into remembering how he had dreamed of putting his hand into the bathroom mirror. Maybe it hadn't exactly been a dream. Or, more likely, he was still dreaming.

'Whatever shows in mirrors is here, and in between

all of the reflections are wild places,' the girl was say-ing, rearranging the bundle in her arms as she spoke.

'Are you trying to say that I came here through my bathroom mirror?' Jack asked. Thinking: this is what comes of eating cold, old, salami pizza before bed.

'I *saw* you,' she said, and gave an impatient flick of her dark hair.

Jack did not know what to say to the girl. It seemed rude to say to somebody that you had dreamed her up. 'What's your name?'

'Names!' she sniffed, rolling her eyes. 'People always want names, don't they? They're mad about naming. I will let the moment name me.' She eyed Jack expectantly.

'You want me to name you?' he asked.

'People from the other side are very dull,' she sighed. 'Give yourself a name for me. I don't need naming for myself, do I?'

This is a dream, Jack reminded himself, but still he felt uncomfortable treating this very definite, rather bossy girl as a figment of his imagination. 'How about Snow White?'

She wrinkled her nose. 'Boring. I should feel as if you were waiting for the dwarfs. Unless you are an overgrown dwarf. Dopey, no doubt.'

He felt rather offended at that, but decided not to show her. 'Alice.'

'Alice?' she mulled. 'Icy, lacy, nice. Yes, that will

do for now. But I might not like it for always. You understand?'

Jack trailed back to the bathroom after her. He found himself looking at his face in the mirror again. Now he was as pale as her.

I look dead, he thought uneasily.

He heard the sound of something right outside the bathroom. Some sort of animal snuffling at the crack under the door, sniffing and whining.

It sounded like a big dog and Jack swallowed uneasily. He was no dog person and dogs always knew it. Unlike Mario, whom Jack's mother had nicknamed the Beastmaster, who would probably be able to tell what breed it was just from its whines, and how old it was by its smell. Then he would open the door and no matter how big or ugly the dog was or how long its teeth were, in seconds it would be writhing on its back with its tongue lolling out redly while Mario rubbed its belly.

Fortunately, Jack didn't have to worry about trying to control it. He glanced over at the girl, wondering why she didn't yell at it to calm down. Then a bolt of fear buried itself in his chest, because she was staring at the door in stark terror.

'What's the matter?' he asked.

'It's a wolver,' she whispered. 'It must have been near when you crossed.'

A long, low, flesh-creeping rumble sounded from

behind the door and all of the hair on Jack's body stood on end because that sound didn't come from any dog.

The scratching grew more ferocious and then there was a thud that made the door shudder on its hinges. Jack imagined something part way between a timber wolf and a wild boar, with razor-sharp tusks and wicked eyes, running at the door and thumping into it, trying to break the lock or maybe smash the wood.

He would not let his mind picture what it would do if it got through the door. Instead, he told himself he was having a salami-pizza nightmare, and that all he had to do to escape was wake up. The whining outside became a wet, furious snarling and after the fourth loud thump, a crack slivered up the wood in the door, flaking the paint.

The girl gave a breathy moan and backed right into the corner furthest from the door. 'You can get away through the mirror, but I can't,' she hissed accusingly, clutching her bundle to her chest.

Jack abandoned any attempt to will himself awake, because even in a nightmare he could not save himself and leave her to be savaged.

'I won't leave you,' he promised.

'You will. You will!' she screamed, shaking her head from side to side in a frenzy of fear.

'No,' Jack said firmly. He kept his own fear in check because she was acting scared enough for both of them. 'Let's get out the window.'

'I'll fall,' Alice whimpered.

'There's nowhere to fall from,' Jack said, and opened the window to show her. *His* bathroom window, his mind said, as he pushed the frosted panels so they would swing out. The hinges creaked like they always did, and Jack gaped.

Instead of the suburban backyard he had expected to see, the window opened onto a shadowy, sloping roof that joined another black, sloping roof and another, all running like frozen waves towards the wall of a much higher building. There was a gap between the two buildings, but it was too narrow for him to see the ground. Above, the sky was pitch black, without a single star. What Jack had taken as the grey of dawn was in fact the gritty upward spill of a security light mounted against the wall of the taller building.

From behind them came a long, terrible, ear-splitting howl muffled only slightly by the door. To Jack's horror, distant answering howls sounded from a dozen different directions.

Alice whimpered again as the door rocked under the impact of another onslaught and the snorting redoubled as if the sound of her fear had excited the creature outside. Jack's heart was thumping so loudly he felt sick, but he made himself pull her to the window. She resisted instinctively until another crack appeared in the door, and then she began to climb awkwardly onto the sill. She wouldn't let Jack hold her bundle but, at his urging, she jumped to the roof below. Jack got out onto the sill, and pulled the window shut behind him, then he jumped too. The roof was spongy and he landed softly, surrounded by the acrid smell of tar.

'Don't dawdle! We have to keep moving,' Alice said sharply.

As if she came up with the plan of climbing out the window instead of me, Jack thought indignantly.

But when she began to run, her feet drumming on the roof, and her sharp-edged shadow stretched out behind her, he followed. They ran to the gap, which was even narrower than it had looked from the bathroom window. Peering warily over the edge into the dark slit, Jack saw the top rungs of a steel ladder cemented into the wall and leading down into the darkness. The security light above only made the darkness below more complete.

'Maybe we ought to stay on the roof,' Jack said. 'There might be more of those things prowling around outside by now and they can't get us up here.'

'Wolvers can go anywhere,' Alice snarled. 'Some of them can climb and there are others that jump like big, pale spiders. They'll come on the roof after us and there's nowhere up here to hide. We'll be trapped.'

She started to climb down the ladder, clutching her bundle under her arm. Jack hesitated because that narrow gap looked exactly like a giant crack in the pavement. Thanks to their mother's stories, Ellen lived in mortal fear of the consequences of treading on cracks, and though Jack had grown out of his own fears, the thought of going into the dark slit brought them back to him.

'Come on,' Alice hissed, vanishing into the darkness below.

A picture of Ellen asleep in her bed came into Jack's mind as he approached the edge of the gap, and as he reached down for the top of the ladder, he seemed to smell the baby powder that she used in play as everything from medicine to fairy dust.

Behind him, there was the sound of shattering glass. A savage howl split the air and Jack heard a heavy thump as something landed on the roof. Terror gave him a brutal push towards the edge and his foot slipped on the rung.

He gave a scream of terror as he fell.

Chapter 3

Jack woke when Ellen prodded him and asked why he was sleeping curled up at the foot of her bed.

Her bed?

Jack looked around himself in astonishment. Legolas regarded him loftily from the *Lord of the Rings* poster over Ellen's bed.

Jack sat up and his head started to pound. How on earth had he got here? He was still in his pyjamas and his feet were like blocks of ice.

The last thing he remembered was going to the toilet; but maybe he had *dreamed* that because the bathroom mirror had swallowed him. Then there had been a house like his, and a girl and some sort of wolves chasing them and he had fallen off a building trying to get away from them.

As a matter of fact, his head felt very much as if he had fallen *on* it.

'I must have sleep-walked,' he told the battered teddy bear jammed between the wall and the bed. Ellen was up and rummaging under the bed for her slippers. He told her about his weird dream while she put on her dressing gown, glossing over the terror of the wolvers so they wouldn't surface in her dreams that night.

'You must have sleep-fallen,' she said, dragging her teddy bear out from behind the bed. 'If you hadn't woken before you hit the ground, you'd have died. That's what Mario says happens.'

'Like he knows,' Jack said, ironically.

But he was thinking that dreams could get you into some pretty oddball situations. Going through the mirror into a world made up of reflections was way out there. It was weird he remembered it so clearly. Usually dreams started to evaporate the minute you tried telling someone about them.

'Hop up. I have to make the bed,' Ellen commanded.

Jack obeyed and his head throbbed. Probably he had slept with his neck twisted around. Or maybe he had bumped into something. But sleepwalking? He had never done that before and he had no idea why he would have come into Ellen's room.

He caught sight of a picture on the dresser and grinned, immediately feeling better. The picture had been taken on a camping holiday that had become a family legend. He was just a little kid and Ellen a toddler. She had been left to sleep in the car while they set up camp, but she was awake by the time they had finished, standing up and gurgling at them through the window, and waving something in her chubby fingers.

Their mother had screamed when she found Ellen had a tight grip on a big decapitated grasshopper. When Jack had asked what had happened to its head, their mother blanched and started fishing in Ellen's mouth. Ellen screamed in protest but in seconds their mother had withdrawn a lump of greenish mush that had once been the grasshopper's head; Jack felt like vomiting and their mother retched, but Ellen just went on screaming indignantly. It was like something out of a horror movie, but it was funny too, and funny all over again when Ellen was old enough to find the story mortifying. He never lost an opportunity to remind her of it.

'Remember when you bit the head off that grass-hopper?' he said now, tapping the picture.

Ellen made a face at him, but she liked it when he teased her. Maybe it comforted her to remember those days.

'How about a bit of grasshopper for breakfast?' he said, grinning. 'Or a big warty cane toad with bulging eyes all covered with river slime?'

Ellen, giggling, began to beat him with the teddy bear.

'Oh, look at this,' Jack said to an invisible audience as he fended her off. 'Look how she's treating poor Mr Foo. But what can you expect of a girl who bites the heads off grasshoppers?' He sprang at her suddenly, and squashed her and Mr Foo together in a bear hug.

Ellen squeaked with delight. She loved it when he pretended to rough her up. Once their father had done it, but he hardly ever touched either of them now.

'Remember the time we were camping and Daddy was a dragon?' Ellen said wistfully. She sat on the bed beside him and smoothed Mr Foo's fur.

Jack nodded, though he wondered if she could really remember back so far or had simply adopted his memories. He remembered it quite clearly. Their father had been giving Ellen a horsy ride and Jack had come over with a stick, saying he was a knight and that he needed the horse to go and kill the dragon.

'*I* am the dragon,' their father said suddenly. 'I have been disguising myself as a horse. Why do you want to kill me?'

Jack had been taken aback, though that was exactly the kind of thing that made games with his father thrilling. He was always introducing something you would never imagine so you had to really think about what you were doing instead of just doing it. You had to be *clever* to play with him, Mario had said in the days when he had sometimes gone away camping with them.

'You have been terrorising the peasants and burning up their fields,' Jack accused.

'That wasn't me,' the dragon protested. 'The fire in that field was lit by a flash of lightning. As for terrorising people, I'm not the one who sits around the fire at night telling stories about evil monsters.'

Jack, who had relished scaring himself and Ellen the night before with just such a story, couldn't help feeling a little embarrassed. 'Everybody knows dragons are evil,' he had defended himself.

'Why? Because I breathe fire? I can't help that. I know I roar, but that's like dogs barking at the moon or kids yelling in a school playground. I'm supposed to roar. I'm harmless but no one believes it because of how fierce-looking I am. Everyone screams when they see me, and knights try to kill me. That's why I disguised myself as a horse so I could play with this little princess . . .'

The dragon's voice had become sadder and sadder and all of a sudden Ellen burst into tears and begged Jack not to kill it. Their mother had gathered her up and commanded the knight and the dragon to make up and be friends because she wasn't having her upset.

Ellen stood up, tucking Mr Foo under her arm. 'I'm having first shower.'

Jack shrugged. Usually he commandeered the bathroom first but this morning he didn't feel like defending his rights as eldest. After Ellen had gone out, he took up the photograph and examined it more closely. In it, they were sitting round the campfire: Ellen on his mother's lap, and Jack on his father's. All of their hands were stacked together like musketeers pledging an oath of loyalty. Their father was laughing, his mouth open as he spoke. Jack was laughing at the sight of the camera propped up on the log. Their mother was, smiling, but her head was turned away slightly as if something had caught her attention at the last minute. Ellen looked as if she was really taking to heart what their father said. Funny thing was, Jack remembered quite clearly what he had been saying.

All for one and one for all. All ways. Always.

At breakfast, Jack watched his father cut up Ellen's toast for the boiled eggs. They both looked so serious.

Ellen always had that funny solemn manner, but once their father had teased her about it, calling her his pint-sized granny. He used to make them laugh at breakfast. Sometimes their mother would pretend to get angry, or sometimes she really got mad, but he always made her laugh in the end, too. Some breakfasts got so hilarious they would become kind of crazy. Jack had occasionally wished his mother and father were a little more like other kids' parents.

One time his mother waved her arms like a helicopter and sent a mug smashing out of his father's hands against the wall. She had burst into tears, and flung herself over the couch.

'I'm a bad mother and a bad wife. I warned you!'

she had yelled at their father.

He had taken her gently into his arms, not caring that her tears stained his shirt, or that she struggled against him. He made a sign for Jack to take Ellen out, and as they left the kitchen they heard him telling their mother that he loved her, and that he would love her forever, no matter what happened.

'My heart belongs to you,' he promised.

'Would you have loved me when I was a girl?'

'I have always loved you. Even before I met you I loved the *idea* of you.'

Some days in that last year, Jack had arrived at school feeling worn out with everything that happened in the mornings.

Now he felt like he was starving for laughter or even for a really loud argument, but there were only poached eggs and toast soldiers, and silence.

It seemed to Jack that the silence between them all came from his father. It was as if he had turned into a silence machine. The kitchen was thick with it and it had overflowed into the whole house. It had got harder and harder to do anything, even to speak. Words would bubble up but all of that silence would push them back and flow down Jack's throat after them, getting inside him.

His father buttered a piece of toast and lifted it to his mouth. He seemed to forget what he was doing then, and he sat frozen for a long moment, before putting the untouched toast back on the plate. He wiped his lips with a napkin.

'I have to leave early today,' he said in a monotonous voice. 'You'll have to walk to school.'

'But, Daddy, what about my science project?' Ellen protested. 'I can't carry it all the way.'

Their father seemed not to hear her. He rose and smoothed down the front of his shirt, then he put on his jacket. Ellen gave Jack a pleading look

'Dad?' Jack said. But their father did not answer or look at him. He had not looked at Jack since the day his wife died.

Because it was my fault, Jack thought, chilled.

Ellen opened her mouth, but Jack shook his head to signal that there would be no use in her trying again. Their father barely spoke with them anymore, but this morning it was as though he had slipped even further away.

They left early for school anyway, because Ellen's project was a big glass pickle jar full of greenish muck, and it was too awkward to carry easily or quickly. Jack did not want to talk about their father and he was trying to think of some other subject when Ellen told him that there was a book in the library about a girl who went through a mirror, just like he had done in his dream.

'*Alice Through the Looking Glass*, it's called,' she said.

Jack blinked in surprise. 'I remember that. It must

be where I got the name for the girl in the dream.'

'You read it?' Ellen asked.

He nodded. 'There's two books. *Through the Looking Glass* and . . .'

'*Alice in Wonderland*. I know,' Ellen said eagerly. 'She goes down a rabbit hole to get into Wonderland and she finds this giant mushroom. If you eat from one side of it you grow big but if you eat from the other side, you get small again.'

'Didn't she shrink because she drank from a bottle that said Drink Me?'

Ellen's forehead wrinkled. 'Maybe the mushroom was through the looking glass. I get them mixed up.'

'Maybe a person could really go through a mirror,' Jack murmured absently, just as the school came in sight. A few kids were playing football on the oval that divided the primary section from the rest of the school.

'In books people can do anything, but not in real life,' Ellen said wistfully.

'Not *anything*,' Jack said. 'They can only do what writers decide they can do. At least in real life you have some say in what happens to you.' The jar slipped and he adjusted his grip. 'What is this anyway? It looks like a jar of green slime.'

'It is,' Ellen said. 'I scraped it out of the gutter. We had to bring something everyone can look at through a microscope. I hope it's enough.'

'A little slime goes a long way,' Jack said.

After Jack had carried the jar safely to Ellen's class-room, he walked across the oval and went to his homeroom to get the books he needed for the first lesson. There were only a few kids around because it was still early and he decided he might as well give his locker a tidy. Stacking books and digging out the furry remnants of sandwiches in greased paper, he thought about his dream because he preferred to think about being chased by monsters than about what was happening to his father. On the other hand, it was unsettling to know his body had gone off and done its own thing while his head was asleep. What if it decided to jump off a skyscraper while his brain was in neutral?

When Mario arrived, Jack told him about the dream. He left Alice out, because for some reason the thought that he had dreamed of a girl embarrassed him. Mario was into girls lately, and though Jack thought about them, he didn't want to actually talk about them or to them.

'You better be careful,' Mario said. 'Sleepwalking is dangerous. You might walk off the edge of a cliff and if someone tried to stop you and woke you up suddenly, you would just drop dead of fright.'

'That's a lie,' Jack said uneasily.

'You hope,' Mario fired back. 'But those wolvers sound sav.' Sav was short for savage and was Mario's latest word for great. 'Pity you didn't actually see

them. You should have looked before you leaped.'
He fell about laughing at himself.

'Very funny. I heard them and that was enough for
me,' Jack said.

He couldn't help laughing, because Mario laughed
exactly like a hyena. He wondered whether that
raucous, merry laughter would have any effect on
the silence in their house. One bit of Jack wanted to
ask Mario over, to see. But at the same time he was
reluctant to expose his father to his friend. Especially
now when he seemed to be getting worse than ever.

It was nearly dark when Jack left the school to go
home. He had stayed back late in the library to do
some research for an assignment he had been putting
off for two weeks, and which was due to be handed
in the next day. The sight of a man walking a fat,
panting corgi reminded him of the wolvers from his
dream and he found himself wishing he had spared
a moment to look behind him to see what they were.
Thinking back he was pretty sure that whatever had
been outside the bathroom had been two-footed, but
Alice had called it a wolver. Maybe it was a wolfish-
looking man. Or a werewolf.

He shuddered.

It had only been a nightmare, of course, but Jack
wished he had been thinking of something less horrible when he came around the corner to the mall
and saw that the shops, the streetlight in the centre
of the mall and the houses beyond them were all in

darkness. That meant there had been a power failure, but it couldn't be a total district blackout because he could see lights a few streets away.

Most likely a car had run into a light pole.

Jack seemed to faintly hear the howling of the wolvers from his nightmare. But he refused to let mere imagination scare him into turning back and skirting the blacked-out area. There was enough moonlight for him to see, he assured himself, striding forward confidently. He even cast a moon shadow, though he didn't much like the way it wavered in front of him and was then swallowed up by the shop shadows.

He didn't look up because the brightness meant there was probably a full moon. His mother said you went mad if you looked at the full moon. Seeing his wide-eyed belief the time she said that, she burst into laughter and said he shouldn't be so gullible.

'Gullible?' Ellen had enquired curiously. 'Is that like seagulls? Or is it that man who was shipwrecked with midgets?'

It wasn't that funny but Jack and his mother had exchanged a startled look before bursting into laughter. Ellen laughed too, though she had no idea why they were laughing. Back then, Ellen thought *laughter* was funny.

Thinking of them all together like that made the darkness of the street less threatening, and some of the confidence Jack had been pretending became real. He savoured the memory, sucking sweetness from it as if it was the last sliver of a piece of chocolate.

'Stop,' their mother had finally begged, flapping her hand like a flag of truce. 'I'll die if I laugh any more.'

It was an odd thing to say, for you would think laughing was one of the few things you couldn't die from. On the other hand, Mario had told them about an uncle of his who laughed so much, his heart burst. Jack could not imagine a more gory death than that. A heart bursting.

All of a sudden, a few steps away, a man-shaped shadow separated from the shop shadows. Jack stopped, his heart pounding, and it flashed across his thoughts that this was a burglar who had somehow stopped the power so he could rob the shops without setting off the burglar alarms.

The man began to turn his head and Jack instinctively sidestepped into the deeper shadows of the nearest doorway. He nearly died when he saw a pair of eyes looking through the window at him, but even as he hitched in a panicky breath to wind a scream, he recognised it was his own reflection.

He listened, letting his schoolbag straps slide slowly down his arm. The bag hit the ground with a soft thud but there was no shout of discovery. Jack told himself he had probably imagined the guy. But another few minutes passed before he could force himself to look out.

To his horror, the man was still there, and he had

dropped into a hunched, half-crouching stance. As Jack watched, the man threw his head back and light glinted on white teeth as if he was baring them to the moon.

A watery sense of terror stole through Jack's limbs and he reeled back and pressed his face to the cold window, knowing it would not save him but not knowing what else to do, as a soft footfall approached his hiding place.

Chapter 4

Fear beat its wings at Jack's ears and he seemed to see his mother's face, beautiful and elusive, peering anxiously at him from behind the dark glass. Then the shop window began to quiver and Jack felt himself being sucked forward into his reflection. He closed his eyes but instead of butting his head on the window, he was falling.

He landed on his stomach, all the wind squashed out of him. His chin had banged against the asphalt, jarring his teeth together horribly. *I might have bitten off my tongue*, he thought, as pain shot through his head and blackness flowed over him in an oily wave.

When he opened his eyes again, Jack found he was lying on his back on the cold cement floor of some sort of tiny, low roofed shed. To his astonishment, the girl from his dreams, Alice, was kneeling nearby with her back to him, staring intently out of a square opening in the wall near the roof.

Bewildered, Jack drew breath to speak but without

turning her head she gave him a hard pinch on the leg and hissed urgently at him to be quiet.

He heard the sounds of growls and movement overhead.

Wolvers, Jack thought.

Alice shifted quickly to the side of the opening as if she feared being seen. Looking around, Jack figured they were in some sort of a storm water drain, and the opening was at street level. It sounded as if a horde of wolvers was pounding back and forth on the path and street above, growling and snarling to one another.

Turning his head the other way, Jack saw that what he had taken for a shadowed wall behind them was a small tunnel running away into darkness. Now that he looked properly he thought he could just make out a round opening at the end of it, where the water would go, but it was too small for a human body.

His heart nearly stopped when he noticed several sets of glowing greenish eyes looking out at him. Alice glanced back and past him.

'Cats,' she said briefly, and made a pinching motion that he took as a warning to be quiet.

Sitting up carefully, he gazed back into the pipe until his eyes adjusted to the darkness. He was amazed to see that Alice was right.

A small thin cat was back there sitting perfectly still, and beside her, for it must be a she, were three tiny trembling kittens. They were all staring at him.

They had to be feral because they were so silent. Mario said wild kittens only survived because they were instinctively quiet.

Then the growling sounds above recalled his fear and confusion. Jack tried to understand what had happened. He had been on his way home and he had seen someone in the mall that scared him. He had hidden in a shop doorway. That was the last thing he remembered clearly.

He shook his head then regretted it as pain shot across the back of his eyes. But it was not in vain for with the sharp ache came the memory of falling and landing hard. He had no idea how he had fallen, but he must have knocked himself out.

Presumably Alice had dragged him into the drain, but how could she exist outside of his dream? Or was it that, having knocked himself out, he was simply continuing the previous night's dream? That happened sometimes and in fact the dream had even ended with him falling. But, in that case, what was happening to him right now in the real world? Was he lying unconscious in the mall with some burglar about to murder him?

More growls and a dragging set of footsteps passed overhead, but then the sounds seemed to recede slightly.

'They smell us,' Alice mouthed, leaning to speak right into his ear. 'They haven't figured out we're under them. The smell ends here so they think we must have gone back up into one of the buildings. They're climbing up to look. We'll have to make a run for it.'

'I don't understand what's happening,' Jack whispered.

'Get ready!' Alice hissed urgently, positioning herself at the opening.

Jack felt sick with fear, but he knelt behind her in readiness because he had the feeling she would just leave him behind if he refused to go.

'Now,' Alice said softly, and scrambled out of the drain opening into the street.

Jack grazed his elbow on the ground in his hurry to go after her. By the time he was on his feet again, she had already sprinted some way down the lane that passed between the two buildings rearing up on either side of them. Jack followed, running as quietly as he could. His head pounded with every step, and his neck crawled at the thought of something reaching out from behind to grab him, but he wasted no time looking over his shoulder.

After five minutes he started to get a stitch. He ignored it, but soon it was like a knife in his side. He was forced to stow down while ahead of him Alice ran on, seemingly tireless. The ragged tail ends of her bundle fluttered behind her.

'Alice,' Jack cried after her, more afraid of being left alone than of seeming weak.

She glared over her shoulder but stopped and

waited until he caught up. 'You must be quiet. They will be back on the ground and find our trail soon enough without your shouting to bring them quicker. And you have to go faster.'

'Usually I'm a good runner, but . . .'

Alice clicked her tongue impatiently. 'We have to get into one of the wild places. The wolvers won't follow us there. You can rest then.'

They heard a wild cry of rage and triumph behind them.

'They come,' Alice shouted. 'Run.' She whirled and started to run faster than ever, no longer trying to be quiet.

Jack ran too, his fear greater than the pain of the stitch, but he could not seem to run very fast. It was as if there were leaden weights on his feet. He kept his eyes fixed on Alice desperately, though she was drawing further and further away from him. He could now hear the noise of the wolvers' pursuit quite clearly. It sounded as if there was a whole pack of them racing along the streets after them, and by their speed they would have him any minute.

Even the horrible thought of their teeth and claws could not make him go faster. Instead, to his horror, Jack found himself slowing down.

Alice stopped again, and looked back at him. 'This way, quickly,' she called, pointing. Then she stepped into what looked like a brick wall, and vanished.

'Wait!' Jack screamed, but there was no answer.

He could hear the grunts and snarls of the wolvers, and knew they must be close enough to see him now. Gasping and stumbling, he nearly missed the narrow lane she had taken. Almost sobbing with relief, he flung himself into what was scarcely more than a gutter between two towering buildings. His shoulders reached from one side to the other, and he had to angle himself so that he could move freely. He prayed the wolvers would be too big to fit after them, and a mere second later, he heard a rage of snapping and furious howling from behind and knew his prayer had been answered. Sweat ran down his body under his T-shirt, though whether he was sweating out of relief or leftover fear he could not tell.

Then, all at once, there was silence.

Only then did he dare to look back. He had only come a few steps along the lane, but it was so shadowy that he could not make out the end in any detail. Nor had he any desire to go back and check, in case the wolvers were waiting for him to do just that. Instead he hastened to catch up to Alice, who was just about to disappear again, for the lane bent gradually away from its straight course.

The brick walls of the buildings had now given way to high fences bordering the lane on either side, and separating it from what must be the yards behind the buildings. Along the top of the fence grew a big dark creeper, with long hanging tendrils, and pale white flowers all sewn together under a silver lace of moonlit spider webs. It was exactly the sort of lane in which you could imagine a crazed drug addict leaping at you, or a vampire.

Alice was striding ahead calmly and Jack wondered at this, for, confronted by wolvers, she had been virtually paralysed with fear. Then an uneasy thought occurred to him.

'They won't think to come around the other end of the lane and wait for us, will they?'

'Thinking is not what wolvers do,' Alice said. 'But even if they did, they couldn't find the other end of this lane. It's one of the paths that lead to the wild places and wolvers don't go into them.' She sounded annoyed and Jack wondered if she blamed him for their predicament. His arrival in her grey land had seemingly brought the wolvers in the first place, but he could not see how he could have avoided whatever it was he had done. How was he to know he would fall through the mirror? Or that it would bring a pack of snarling creatures after him?

'What are wolvers, anyway?' he asked.

'You ask a lot of questions,' Alice said disapprovingly, rearranging her ragged bundle. Jack had thought it was just a bundle of clothing or sheets, but now he could see there was something solid inside the rags and he wondered what it could be. Clearly it was valuable to Alice for she never let it out of her sight or laid it aside for more than a moment.

'The wolvers smelled your coming,' she said, as

the lane began to slope steeply uphill and curve to the left.

It was not really an answer, but Alice never seemed to answer questions properly.

'What do they do when they catch people who come through the minor?' Jack asked, deciding to approach the question from another direction. Perhaps the wolvers were merely some nightmarish form of guard dog but, if so, who had set them the task of guarding the borders of the greylands? Something else occurred to him. 'If the wolvers smell people who come through the mirror, why are *you* running away from them? You didn't come through the mirror, did you?'

Alice stopped without warning and turned to stare at Jack so intently that he had the feeling she was really seeing him properly for the first time. 'I have something they want and, coming after you, they have got scent of it as well,' she said at last. She gave him a sly, flickering smile and her gaze dropped to her bundle.

'What's in it?' Jack asked.

Her expression changed abruptly. 'You can't have it,' she hissed, and backed away with her spare hand curled into a claw, as if she feared he meant to attack her and steal the bundle.

'I don't want it,' Jack assured her quickly.

Alice eyed him mistrustfully. 'Why did you ask about it then?'

'I was just curious about why the wolvers would want . . . whatever it is.'

'Curiosity is dangerous here.' Alice turned to walk on. 'You'd best go back where you came from before it gets you into trouble,' she added distantly, without looking over her shoulder.

It occurred to Jack that, in a way, she was telling him to wake up out of the dream. Weird! 'What if I don't want to go back?' he asked, to see how she would react. 'I could just stay in these wild places.'

'No one can stay in them for long,' Alice said. 'Everything is changing all the time. Everything shifts and shivers from one form to another. Nothing is certain. You would have to come out sooner or later, and when you did, the wolvers would smell you. They'd find you eventually, no matter how good you were at hiding.'

'They haven't found you.' Jack felt indignantly that she was implying she was better at hiding than he was.

'They can't smell me out because I belong here,' Alice pointed out. 'They can smell this, though.' She nodded at the bundle. 'But only when they're close to it.'

She looked so suspicious again that Jack decided not to ask any more questions about the bundle for the time being. 'Would they eat me if they got me?' he asked instead.

To his surprise, she shook her head. 'They would

take you to the grey tower and you'd end up with wings.'

'*Wings!*' Jack gasped. Even the word on his lips seemed to fizz.

Alice gave him a sour smile. 'Don't get too excited. They're not that wonderful.'

'But wings,' Jack could only sigh. How could having wings not be wonderful? Fairies and angels had wings! If he hadn't loved the sheer enchantment of the idea that he could have wings, he would have loved it because of his mother always saying she had hidden wings.

'I would love to have wings,' he said at last, almost exhausted by the wave of longing that had flowed through him.

'Why did you run from the wolvers, then?' Alice asked.

'I didn't know they would give me wings. You didn't say so and anyway it didn't sound like that was what they wanted to do to me.' Jack wondered suddenly if 'getting wings' was Alice's way of saying 'dead'.

'The wings . . .' he stammered, not knowing how to phrase it. 'Are they *real* wings?'

'Real enough,' Alice said, and patted her hump suggestively. 'You don't get them right away, though. They have to grow and once they do, you can't go back through the mirror. Never. You'd have to stay here forever.'

Jack stared at Alice, in wonder that she could have wings under her cloak. But then he doubted it. After all, why cover them if she had them? And although there was something attractive about her, despite her bad tempers and prickly manner, he had the feeling she sometimes said whatever came into her head. Most likely she pretended for her own comfort that her hump was a set of wings.

'You don't believe me,' she said sullenly.

'I just don't understand why the wolvers would chase after me to give *me* wings.'

'They do not *give* them. No one *gives* wings. The wolvers take those they capture to the grey tower where wings are to be got.'

'Someone in the grey tower gives them out?' Obviously this grey tower must be some sort of authority in the greylands.

'Wings are got from the grey tower,' Alice repeated obscurely.

'Okay, but why do the wolvers take people they capture there? Do they get a reward for it?'

Alice laughed. 'Wolvers do not want wings for you or any other. They sniff wanting and it drives them mad. They smelled your wanting as soon as you came, and that is why they are so angry. After the wings grow, there is no more smell of wanting and the wolvers can be at peace. That is their reward, I suppose. At any rate, it is what they want, if wanting nothing can be called wanting.'

She frowned as if puzzling out the intricacies of her own words, and Jack studied the bundle furtively, wondering what was in it to make the wolvers smell it, if they only smelled wanting.

Alice's eyes glittered and she stared into his eyes with sudden coldness. 'I smell *your* wanting now.' She held the bundle protectively to her chest.

'I don't want it,' Jack said firmly. 'I just want to know why the wolvers would want to take it to this grey tower.'

'Wanting to know is the same as any other kind of wanting,' Alice sneered. 'And the wolvers would not bring what I carry to the tower. They would destroy it.'

'Why . . .? Okay, forget it,' Jack said quickly, for Alice had begun to walk faster and he feared she might suddenly run away. 'Just tell me why the wolvers are chasing *me* since I didn't come here wanting anything.'

'But you want wings,' Alice said slyly. 'You said so. *I would love wings.* Even the words smell of wanting.'

'I'm not saying I wouldn't want them,' Jack stammered. 'But those wolvers were after me before I ever thought about wings or knew it might be possible to get them.'

'Wolvers can smell a longing which is not even known to the one who longs,' Alice said.

Jack gave up trying to get information about the wolvers. 'How do you know you can't get back through the mirror with wings?' he asked, determined to make her say outright that she had them if she did.

'Practically everyone who gets them tries to go back because they want to smell things and see colour and hear loud noises again after a while,' she answered evasively. 'But there is no going back once you have wings.' She smiled suddenly, showing her white teeth.

Not a very nice smile, Jack found himself thinking. But she was right about it being quiet as well as colourless. It was not so much silent, as that all sounds were slightly muffled. Truly it was a grey land in all senses.

The lane now curled very tightly into itself and it seemed to go from being a lane to almost a spiralling ramp. This seemed impossible, but before Jack could figure out why, he saw that the lane ended a short way ahead. It was dark and shadowed, but whatever lay beyond was darker still. In fact, it almost looked like solid blackness.

'Is it a mist?' he wondered, for as they came nearer the darkness swirled and shuddered like the skin of some great, black beast.

'I don't know what it is except that it is some sort of wild stuff,' Alice said.

'I don't see how we can go through it,' he said, as they stood side by side gazing into the swirling blackness. No wonder no one stayed for long in the wild places if this was how they looked. 'Maybe we should go back. The wolvers are sure to have gone by now.'

'No one can predict what the wolvers will do,' Alice said. 'Besides, there is no going back. If you turned and walked back now, you would only find another wildness at the other end.'

'Maybe it would be different,' Jack said in a low voice. He really did not think he could bring himself to step into the blackness. It looked as thick as liquid, and maybe he would drown in it.

Alice said calmly, 'The wild places are all different, but turning away from one out of fear usually leads to something worse. Better to go on.'

Jack wondered what could possibly be worse than this. Alice shrugged and said he could go back if he wanted, but she would go on.

Leave me alone here? He wanted to cry, aghast, but he managed to restrain himself. Alice gave him a knowing smile and stepped into the blackness. At least she did not fall away screaming, as if from a precipice, but a dark skein of smoke flowed between them. Steeling himself, Jack followed her. Darkness fell over him like a thick curtain, but there was solid ground underfoot and he could breathe, though the air felt thick and close.

'Come on.' Alice's voice sounded flat and far

away. She was barely visible in the bit of light re-flected from the lane, though they were standing face to face. She shifted the bundle into one arm and held out her hand. Jack took it, thinking she meant to comfort him, but she kept hold of it and turned to go, leading him. A few steps later he understood she had taken his hand out of simple necessity, for the light grew more and more faint, and very soon they were walking in pitch darkness. If they had not held hands, they would certainly have been separated. Jack made no attempt to talk, because he had the creepy feeling that something might be watching them from the darkness.

'Look,' Alice said, her voice sounding thin as if the black air devoured sound as well as light.

Jack looked around fearfully, and his heart gave a quick beat of fright when he saw a set of yellow eyes looming beside them.

'It's just a big cat of some kind,' Alice told him, and she smiled. 'Cats come through the mirrors all the time.'

Jack hardly heard what she was saying because it dawned on him that he had *seen* her smile, though there was no light. Studying her, he found with amazement that she was very faintly luminous. He lifted his own free hand, but it was dull, except for a slight reflected sheen from Alice. Fascinated, he stared at her and only then saw that it was not Alice glowing, but whatever she carried in the bundle. She seemed not to be aware of the light shining on her pale skin and Jack decided to say nothing in case she grew angry at his mentioning the bundle again. He could not think of anything more horrible than being left alone in the darkness. Better not even to think of the bundle since Alice might interpret this as 'wanting'. He didn't want to possess it, though. He just wanted to know what it was, and that wasn't the same thing, no matter what she said.

They seemed to walk for a very long time, and Jack grew steadily colder. This was so gradual, however, that it wasn't until he stumbled that he became aware he could no longer feel his feet. He was shivering uncontrollably, and the thought of being lost in an endless *freezing* blackness terrified him! He did not dare to ask the question on his lips for fear of the answer.

What if Alice was lost and they couldn't find a way out?

The only thing that reassured him was her calmness. She did not act like someone who was lost. He suspected she had taken refuge enough times in these wild places to know her way in and out of them. He got the impression that the wolvers were often after her, and wondered how long she had carried the bundle about with her.

She glanced at him, and he was afraid she might somehow have divined his thoughts. 'How much further?' He blurted out the question as a distraction.

'I don't know,' she said.

Jack gave up trying to talk and concentrated on putting one foot in front of the other. The cold sapped his will and he became strangely sleepy. After a while, it was too much effort to keep his eyes open. There was nothing but blackness to see around them, and anyway, Alice was leading him along like a blind person. Once his eyes were closed, oddly, he felt warmer. And though it was still black, this was a familiar blackness with its little flares of light and squiggles. He sank into the blackness.

Chapter 5

Jack felt his hand being squeezed and forced his eyes open.

He was half lying on the couch and Ellen was pulling at his hand.

'Don't go to sleep, Jack. You promised to read me a story after I brushed my teeth.'

'I . . . I was dreaming,' he said, and licked his dry lips. 'Of . . . of that girl Alice again. I was with her in the greylands.' He felt incredibly disoriented as if he really had been walking through some black place for hours and hours. He even felt cold.

Ellen gave him a severe look as if he had offered his dream as a way of evading a bedtime story. 'You promised.'

Jack struggled to sit up and rubbed at his eyes trying to wake up properly. He felt almost groggy and it was terribly hard to keep his eyes open. 'All right, I'm coming. You go and get into bed. I promise!' he added forcefully as she gave him a look of reproachful doubt.

She went out leaving the book she had brought.

Jack stretched and yawned and scratched his head, trying to remember what he had been doing before he fell asleep, but the dream was too vividly fresh in his mind. Ellen called from her bedroom to say she was in bed already. Jack sighed and stood, picking up the book. It was a very old fairy tale book that had belonged to their mother. Ellen had heard most of the stories before, of course, but she liked hearing her favourites over and over again.

Jack or their father had always read to her, because their mother had not been very good at reading. She could pretend to be anything when they were playing, but when she read words out of a book, her voice had become dull and lifeless. So she had always sat cuddled with Ellen while he or their father read to them. Jack liked reading, liked putting on voices for all of the parts.

Usually Ellen chose which story to read but as he entered her bedroom, Jack said on impulse, 'Shall I read about the Snow Queen?' He had remembered there was a mirror in that story.

Ellen nodded, lying back on her pillow and arranging Mr Foo so that his lopsided head rested beside hers. Jack's mind wandered and his eyes grew heavy. He tried to recall how many times he had dreamed of Alice and her grey land. He found he couldn't remember . . .

Ellen poked at his leg, ordering him to start.

Obediently, Jack found the page.

'Once there was a goblin who had a mirror that would make everything beautiful reflected in it small and unnoticeable, and anything that was ugly stand out very clearly and look much worse than it really was.'

'Where did he get the mirror?' Ellen asked.

She always asked questions. Maybe that was why stories could be read over and over to her and she wouldn't get bored: the answers to her questions couldn't come out of the book. Whoever was reading had to think them up. Usually Jack was good at it, but tonight he felt dull. Maybe he was coming down with something. He still felt cold but he couldn't be bothered getting a coat.

Jack made himself concentrate on Ellen's question. 'Maybe his goblin father gave the mirror to him. Anyway, in this mirror, the most beautiful landscapes looked like boiled spinach. One day the goblin dropped the mirror and it smashed into a thousand million pieces. The wind blew the bits of mirror all over the world . . .'

'All of the four winds blew it,' Ellen said dreamily. Then she frowned. 'If you went through *that* mirror you would be changed into something ugly and bad.'

Startled, Jack looked up from the book. Clearly she remembered him telling her about going through the bathroom mirror in his dream. He wondered if he had scared her.

'We can read something else if you like.'

But Ellen was studying the picture in the book of the goblin gloating over his enchanted treasure. 'That's a bad mirror,' she said, nodding at it. 'Mirrors should only show good things.'

'But then they would be telling lies, because not everything is good,' Jack said.

'Mama told me mirrors tell lies.'

'She might have been playing,' he said. 'You know how she always played that things were real and sometimes they weren't?'

'Mama wasn't playing. She was scared,' Ellen said solemnly. 'Mr Foo is scared, but I'm not. Go on. I want to hear the rest.'

Jack returned to the book.

'The mirror had broken into millions of pieces and the wind blew them all over the world. If a person got a speck in their eye, the person would only see the ugly side of things from then on, but if a piece got in their blood and it reached their heart, it would freeze into a solid block of ice and they couldn't feel anything anymore.'

'They were cold,' Ellen said.

'No, they weren't cold or hot because they couldn't feel anything. That's what happened to them. They became numb.'

'Numb, so they couldn't feel anything even if you pinched them hard,' Ellen said told Mr Foo.

'There were a boy and a girl who loved one another very much, living in a village,' Jack read.

'What were their names?' Ellen asked, her eyes drooping.

'The boy's name was Kay and the girl was Gerda. One day they were sitting in the garden when Kay cried out, "Ow! Something has stung my heart . . ."'

Jack broke off and when Ellen did not speak, he looked at her. She was fast asleep. He closed the book, stood up and tucked the bedclothes up around her, making sure Mr Foo was covered as well. He kissed her pink cheek and she sighed her minty toothpaste into his face.

Jack went into the kitchen. His father was an island in the middle of a sea of paper. He was not writing or reading anything. He was just staring at the wall.

'Dad, can I talk to you?' Jack suddenly made up his mind to ask if he could invite Mario around.

'Go to bed,' his father said, without looking at him.

Jack felt as if he had been slapped. Without a word, he turned and left the kitchen. Once he had talked with his father, but now it was all shut up, go away, be quiet. Jack had the feeling his father would not have cared and might not even have noticed if he really did go through a mirror and never came back.

'But Ellen would care,' Jack told his reflection in the bathroom mirror.

He cleaned his teeth then went into his room, thinking he should do his homework, but feeling strangely thickheaded and tired. The bedroom was freezing and he realised he must have left the window open. As he went to shut it, something streaked across the room and flew out over the sill. A bird? He leaned out the window. A grey cat sat on the lawn below the window looking up at him. It was little more than a kitten, and very skinny.

'You want some milk, puss?' Jack called down softly, but at the sound of his voice, the cat turned tail and vanished into the darkness.

The curtains flapped at Jack, brushing his cheeks as he closed the window, and he decided it was too cold to work. He was too tired to think straight anyway. Tugging off his jeans and socks, he climbed into bed, but he could not seem to get warm despite the covers drawn up around his neck. He huddled into a ball and put his head under the blankets, but even surrounded by his own warm breath, he still felt freezing. After some time, he drifted into a light doze. He dreamed he was a small boy walking hand in hand along a sunny shore with his mother.

She shook his hand and told him not to fall asleep. 'I'm awake,' he mumbled, though his eyes had fallen shut. It took all of his will to open them.

Alice was peering into his face and he found it was her hand he was holding. 'You don't look awake,' she said sharply. 'You mustn't go to sleep in the wild places or you'll never wake up.'

Jack blinked at her stupidly. What was happening?

He must be dreaming again. Or had he been dreaming of Ellen? It was too confusing and he was so terribly cold.

'Look,' Alice said, nodding.

Ahead in the distance there was light, as at the end of a very long tunnel.

'Is it the end?' Jack asked, or tried to ask, but all that came out of his frozen lips was an inaudible croak.

Yet Alice seemed to understand. 'Perhaps,' she said. 'If it is, we will be lucky, for some of the wild places are very large and there is more than one part to them. Once I was in a stony place wandering for many weeks, or maybe months, before I could come to the end of it.'

Jack was too cold even to feel despair at her words. His brain was frozen and so were his emotions. He stumbled towards the light, barely conscious that Alice had let go of his hand. It was as if there was a string pulling him towards the brightness, and that was all he knew, though it was a long time before they came any closer to it. When they did, Jack saw they had not come out into the open, as he had hoped, but to a cave filled with luminous mist.

Warm air flowed from its mouth and Jack collapsed against the black, smooth rocks at the entrance and turned to face the heat. 'I have to rest,' he rasped, feeling as if he would never be warm again.

Alice gave him a look of scorn. 'You should not

have let yourself go to sleep.'

When Jack said nothing, she sat down. She did not look tired or cold, and she did not put her bundle down. 'We must go soon,' she muttered as if to herself. 'It's bad for things that belong on the other side of the mirror to be in the wild places for too long.' She stroked the bundle of rags tenderly, and a strange thought entered Jack's chilled mind.

'Is that from the other side of the mirror, too?' he asked, before he could stop himself.

Alice only nodded, seeming so mesmerised by the movements of her hand over the bundle that for once she did not take his mention of it as an expression of secret wanting.

Growing warmer, Jack decided to chance another question. 'How did you get it through the mirror?'

Alice leapt to her feet, eyes flaring with outrage. 'It's none of your business! I didn't steal it, if that's what you think. It was a gift and I can take it anywhere I want. It belongs to me.'

Jack said swiftly, 'But it's in danger here. You said so yourself. The wolvers want to destroy it and the only way to escape them is to hide in here, and now you say that's dangerous, too.'

Alice's fury dissolved into confusion and a kind of despair. 'What else can I do? It belongs to me. It wants to stay with me.'

Jack pounced on her words. 'It *wants*? Isn't that exactly why the wolvers can smell it?' Then he realised what he had said, and he asked, 'Is it something *alive*?'

But now he had gone too far. Fear flashed across Alice's face and she began to edge towards the cave opening. Seeing her intention to dash by him, Jack held up his hands. 'Please, don't leave me here, Alice. I don't mean to upset you. It's just that you always act so mysterious and I don't know what's happening to me. I promise I don't want your bundle.'

She hesitated and then said fiercely, 'Promise? You promise it?'

He nodded solemnly. 'I promise. I'll never take it from you or touch it without your permission.' The outrage faded slowly from Alice's white face, and now, strangely, she looked as if she was going to cry. Jack hated it when people wept. He never knew what to do. 'Hey, you realise you don't know my name yet?' he said, trying to distract her.

Alice did not respond. She was again stroking the bundle in her arms, her expression morose.

'I'm Jack,' he went on determinedly and held out his hand. A wary look flitted over her pale features, but after a hesitation, she put her hand out too, and Jack shook it very gently. It felt small and defenseless, like Ellen's, and he wished he might go on holding it as he had done earlier. But she soon pulled it away.

'We should go,' she said briskly. And with that, she walked past him into the cave. Jack followed quickly in case she changed her mind. Her shoulders drooped and he saw her black mood in them and decided to hold his tongue until they got out of the wild place.

If they got out, a little voice in his mind whispered treacherously.

He ignored it. At least he was warm and there was light now.

The cave had grown wider and higher and Jack could no longer see the walls. There was only the swirling, creamy mist.

It was so damp he thought it must be steam and maybe that was why it felt warm. His hands and face were clammy with moisture, and the ends of his hair stuck damply to his forehead.

He noticed suddenly that over to one side the mist had thickened into whipped cream and here and there, scattered though it, were luminous grey arches. It took Jack a full minute to realise that what he was looking at were *colourless rainbows*.

'Look,' he murmured and pointed.

'Reflections of light on water,' Alice said, sounding pleased, though she was still frowning. 'I told you, everything here comes from reflections of the other side. But we're in luck to find this in a wild place.'

'What do you mean? Is it the way out?' Jack asked, as she changed direction and hurried towards the arches.

'It is *a* way out, but not for long. Hurry,' she urged, and jumped into the rainbow mist.

Jack gasped as she vanished, then ran forward and jumped after her.

He landed beside Alice in a city street. It was as if the swirling mists and the rainbows were no more than a thin curtain he had leapt through. The street was colourless like everything else in the greylands, but after the mists, it seemed very bright. He turned to find there was nothing behind them but a cloud of steam in front of a brick wall and already it was beginning to evaporate.

'Rainbows come and go on the other side and it's the same here,' Alice said. 'Mirrors stay unless they get moved or broken. Then that bit of the world changes, or it breaks into pieces. If you're in them you get broken or shifted, too.'

No wonder you got seven years bad luck for breaking a mirror! Jack thought.

He turned to study their new surrounds more closely. The street they had come into was like something out of a history book, for the road they were standing on was narrow and made of grey cobblestones worn smooth as if dozens of feet and carriages had run over them. On either side of it were tall houses all built leaning against one another. Most of them hid their feet behind little walls, and they all had steeply shingled roofs and clusters of very small, square windows bracketed by shutters. Some had window boxes complete with grey flowers.

Down the street the way widened into a square and in the centre of it was an old-fashioned stone well.

'It's like something out of a story book,' Jack said, thinking the well looked like something out of his mother's fairy tale book. Wasn't it even the very well beside which the goblin dropped and broke his magic mirror?

'Books,' Alice echoed darkly. Her eyes travelled swiftly up and down the street. 'I can't stay here anymore. The wolvers will come after you again when they pick up your scent.'

Jack stared at her. 'But you can't leave me here.'

'Why not?' she demanded, scowling. 'I didn't ask you to come. I'm not responsible. I don't know why you're here if you don't want to stay. Why didn't you go back at once?'

'I would have but the wolvers came and I didn't want to leave you alone,' Jack said indignantly.

Alice glared at him. 'Don't try and blame me.'

Jack made himself calm down. 'I'm not blaming you. I just need to know how to get back home.'

'You'll have to find another mirror,' Alice said sulkily.

'Will it bring me back near home?' Jack asked. 'I wouldn't want to come out in some faraway place.'

'I have to go,' Alice said sharply. 'The wolvers will come soon.' She glanced at the bundle with fleeting anxiety.

'What will I do if they come?' Jack heard the

desperation in his voice. 'I don't know how to find one of those paths to the wild places, and even if I managed it, I wouldn't know how to get out again once I was in.'

'You can follow the cats,' Alice said.

'Alice . . .'

'I have to go now,' she said in a hard little voice, and Jack saw there was no point in pleading.

All at once a sobbing growl rent the silence. It was not the mindlessly savage wolver's cry but something else. Jack thought it was as if some terrible monster was dying in agony.

After a long, long moment, the sound faded, though the air seemed still to throb with the awful anguish of it.

'What was *that*?' he whispered.

Chapter 6

'That was the laughing beast,' Alice said in a hushed voice. Her face was pinched with fear.

Jack was stunned. Could that tortured roar really have been *laughter*?

'*What* is a laughing beast?' he asked.

Alice pressed her lips into a thin slit and shuddered.

'Well . . . is it dangerous?'

'It's dangerous for things that belong here. Even the wolvers fear it.'

'But I'm not from here.'

'I don't know what it would do to you,' Alice muttered. 'But anyway it's in a cage. You'll be safe if you stay away from it.'

'What harm can it do caged?'

'I won't answer any more of your questions,' Alice shouted. 'I have to go.'

'Couldn't I come with you?' Jack begged, reaching out.

Alice slapped his hand away, and he saw she thought he was trying to snatch her bundle. Suddenly he felt weary from trying to reassure her. Perhaps it was impossible to reassure someone whose fear was so great. He let his hand fall away. He wanted to tell her she was nothing more than a creature in his dream, and since it was *his* dream she had to do what he wanted. But dreamers didn't decide what to dream. Dreams did what they liked to their dreamers and he was no more master of what was happening than she.

Alice began to walk away, looking back at him warily every few steps as if she thought he might run after her and catch hold of her. But he just stood watching her go. After a while she stopped looking back and walked faster.

Jack watched until she was out of sight, half hoping she would change her mind and come back, but she didn't. So he took a deep breath and looked around, wondering what he ought to do. He wanted to go home, but he wasn't sure how that could be done. Alice had said to find a mirror, but even if he could, she hadn't answered when he asked where it would it bring him out. Maybe he would end up on the other side of the world. What if he came out in a place where they spoke another language? He could look for a mirror that was in a place that looked like somewhere from home, but how long would that take? There must be millions and millions of reflections in the world.

The street Alice had gone down went up in the other direction to the top of a small hill. Jack decided to walk up it and see if he could spot anything that looked familiar. But he would have to be careful no matter which way he went. There were the wolvers and he didn't like the sound of the laughing beast for all that Alice had sworn it was caged. Maybe she had said that just to be rid of him.

It only took a few minutes to reach the summit of the hill. Unlike the cobbled street on the other side, the road he now saw was quite ordinary and modern. It was surfaced in dark bitumen and further down it were a lot of buildings that looked like factories. Past them was a suburban cluster of houses.

There was not a single person in sight, nor the sound of any car or machine. Jack might have stepped inside a black-and-white photograph.

He debated whether to go in the direction of the factories and look for mirrors in the houses beyond, or to turn back and go the same way as Alice. Part of him wanted to follow her to pay her out for leaving him, but another part of him said to let her alone. After all he had soured her mood by saying she was putting her precious bundle in danger. And he couldn't help remembering how nicely she had held his hand and led him through the darkness. She was a peculiar girl and maybe a little mad, but perhaps she had done the best she could for him. At least she had not left him wandering in the dark.

With this thought, he began to walk towards the factories.

He found himself wondering again what Alice had in her bundle. She claimed it was a gift and that it wanted to be with her, but something in the defiant way she had said it made him think that might not be exactly true. Her saying it wanted to be with her made him certain there must be something alive in it: maybe some animal. But it would certainly have suffocated, all wrapped up in rags, and besides, what kind of animal shone the way it had in the dark? He had reached the first factory, which was enclosed by a high mesh fence. The front gates were locked and had coils of barbed wire along the top, but there was a smaller gate standing open beside them. Inside were a lot of big warehouses facing a central yard. All of their doors were wide open but it was too dim to see inside.

Out of the corner of his eye, Jack saw something dart through the doorway of the nearest warehouse and he froze, thinking it might be a wolver. But the wolvers were noisy and they had no reason to hide from him. Whatever had run into the warehouse seemed to have no more wish to be seen than he did. Curiosity was dangerous, Jack told himself firmly, but he was unable to resist going through the gate to look inside.

He was half disappointed to find there was nothing but a lot of old machinery sitting around. He caught sight of a black tail flitting under a bench and realised he had seen a cat. Alice said there were lots of them in the greylands.

Somehow that didn't surprise him. Mario always said cats had strange powers.

Jack crouched down and peered under the bench. Two pale-green points of light glimmered at him and it struck him suddenly that all of the cats he had seen in the greylands had *coloured* eyes, though the rest of them appeared to be as black and white and grey as everything else. Was that because they didn't belong here? Remembering the cat he had surprised in his bedroom, and Alice's suggestion that he follow a cat if he wanted to get back through the mirrors, Jack wondered if cats might not somehow be the key to getting home.

'Puss puss,' he called softly.

The cat did not move.

'Puss,' he crooned. 'Good puss. Get me out of this and I'll give you a whole bowl of eggs and cream.' He inched his way towards the bench, but without warning the cat sprang out and darted away.

Jack sat back on his heels glumly, but when he rose and turned, the cat was sitting in the doorway of the warehouse calmly watching him.

'Oh, now you're sorry you ran away and you'd like that cream after all?' he asked wryly.

The cat began to wash its paw fastidiously, without taking its green eyes off him. Jack had the uncanny feeling that it was waiting for him, and on impulse he gestured for it to lead the way. To his amazement, it stretched and with a final enigmatic look, walked out into the open.

Jack came outside and found the cat was making its way along the side of the warehouse, heading away from the gate and the road. It glanced back as if to be sure he was following.

'You wouldn't lead me on, would you?' he called softly, coming after it.

It disappeared behind the warehouse, and Jack followed, wryly mindful of the day Mario had the idea they should find out what cats really did with their time. They had traipsed and climbed and run after his grey tomcat for three hours before giving up, exhausted. Leaping effortlessly onto yet another fence, the big cat had stretched itself out above the two exhausted detectives, leaving Jack with the distinct impression that it had deliberately led them on a wild goose chase for its amusement. Mario agreed it might have done because cats were the only animals with a sense of humour. He said it went with their ability to be cruel and for that reason made them more like humans.

Behind the warehouse, Jack found the cat had veered towards the outer fence line. Again it glanced back as if hurrying him on.

'I can't get through that, puss,' he began, and then noticed it was making for a part of the hurricane fence that had come away from its iron frame. It slipped through the gap with an elegant twitch of its tail, and Jack awkwardly eased himself after it. He found himself standing in a field overgrown with weeds and rough grasses that ran the whole way along the back of the factories to the suburb beyond.

In the other direction, it stretched away to a bank of earth that ran parallel to the road. The bank was too high for him to see what lay on the other side.

The cat was picking its way towards it.

'I hope you're not leading me into another wild place,' Jack said, scrambling over prickly brush and sharp grasses. 'I wouldn't mind knowing where one is, but I'm sure not in a hurry . . .'

He stopped, for now he could see that just past the bank the ground dropped away into a long slope covered with rough low bushes. The slope ran down to a small flat valley where a cluster of tents and caravans had been set up. It looked like some sort of fête or bazaar. Beyond the tents the ground rose up steeply again, and was heavily covered with trees.

The cat was sitting on the bank, watching him.

Jack reached out absently and patted it, then was surprised it had let him. He scratched it under the chin and it tilted its head up and purred loudly. It was a she-cat, Jack could see now, and wondered if it could possibly be the cat from in the drain. That had green eyes too, but if so, where were its kittens?

'What have you brought me to?' he asked softly.

The cat yawned delicately.

Jack looked back down at the bazaar. Making up

his mind to have a closer look, he gave the cat a final pat before making his way down the slope. It made no effort to follow, and he wondered if it had really led him here.

When he reached the foot of the hill, he could see that there were tarpaulins on poles over trestle tables piled up with fish and potatoes. This meant it was more a market than a bazaar. It occurred to him that he had not eaten or drunk anything for ages, but although he felt rather empty, he was not really hungry. That was weird because he was *always* hungry. There were some stalls out in the open piled high with masses of grey and white flowers in tubs and Jack thought how unnatural it was to see flowers without colour or scent. They were like the ghosts of flowers. In fact the whole of the greylands was like a ghost of the real world. There was no sign of stallholders or customers but that was not surprising. Jack had seen no one but Alice since he had come here. She had said everyone tried to go through the mirrors after a while, but who was everyone? *Where* was everyone?

Seeing that some of the stalls sold clothes, it came to Jack that there was sure to be a mirror here. He hardly knew what he would do if he found one, but he might as well look. Since there was no one to stop him, he simply slipped between and behind the stalls and trestles, poking in tents and peering under benches. Finally he came to a table piled high with folded blankets and bolts of fabric. There were also dresses and rough-looking shirts in a big heap, and right behind them was a small round tent with a peaked roof.

In some uncanny way, Jack knew that there was a mirror in it.

His heart began to thump. Maybe he could get home through the mirror. Or maybe simply seeing a mirror would wake him, if he were dreaming. He went through the striped flaps into the tent booth. It seemed much bigger than from outside; but there was nothing in it except a mirror. Not at all the kind of mirror you would think to find in a market, it was very big and thick with cloudy glass and a fancy old-fashioned frame. You couldn't see that in the reflection, though. All you could see were the folds and cloth of the tent. There was no way to tell what it corresponded with on the other side.

He reached out and touched the glass, wondering if he ought to say 'open sesame' or something. The mirror didn't ripple and he didn't wake up. Nothing happened, except that his fingers left a hot smear. He shrugged, trying to ignore the fact that he looked crestfallen. He came back out of the tent feeling depressed. He told himself that he should eat something while he had the chance. But in lots of stories, eating food was the means of binding you. In the land of faerie you would be trapped there forever once you ate food of that realm, and in other stories, an enemy would have to protect you if you ate salt with them, because it was a matter of honour.

'What would happen if I ate something?' he wondered out loud. 'Would I be like Sleeping Beauty and never wake again?'

'Ahh, but she was woken with a kiss, though it was a hundred years in coming,' said a rich creamy voice. 'Maybe it was worth the wait.'

Jack spun around in fright, but he couldn't see anything except a lot of wagons and utes and cars parked close together.

'I'm here. Right here in front of you. Don't you see me?'

Jack squinted and saw that amongst the wagons there was an enormous cage. At a glimpse, he had thought it a wagon too, because its back and roof and the sides were closed in with metal sheets decorated in faded stencils, and it had wheels. But on one side, the wagon cage had bars, and through them he saw that something moving. Jack drew nearer but he could barely make out what was inside. It was surrounded and concealed by shadows as if it grew them instead of fur. He thought he saw the vague outline of an enormous shaggy man, but it might just as well have been a strangely dark and dusky bear. Only its eyes were distinct: great, black, shining orbs with silver flecks.

Then he guessed what he was looking at. 'You're the laughing beast!'

'That name was given to me,' the shadowy shape admitted with a ponderous chuckle that was more than anything else a throb of misery. 'It formed me as you see me. Once I was free and nameless and formless as the wind, but now look. This is what comes of naming, you see.' It gestured at the bars and Jack saw a flash of ivory claws.

'Why are you here?' he asked, making sure not to be too close in case it reached out and grabbed him. It must be somewhat wild if it was caged, after all.

'I was put here in the bazaar, though, as you see, I do not belong amongst these dull pears and man-goes,' it said. 'They hoped I might become like these fruits after a time, perhaps, all frowzy rind and silent pips. I was with the circus before that, and though I did not belong there either, it seemed a place that would take in such oddities as could belong nowhere else. I thought I would be able to stay and perhaps even play a useful role. They caged me so as to create a sensation. That made me fearsome, for once I was caged I knew the truth about myself and, knowing, I became dangerous. I scared all of their customers away. It is a strange thing. When I was not caged, no one was afraid of me. But the minute I was behind bars, people kept their distance, just as you are doing. It was the cage that made them afraid. It set their imagination aflame. In the end, they would not let me stay, even caged.'

'Did you bite someone?' Jack enquired.

'I laughed at people,' the laughing beast said. 'My laughter has sharper teeth than any dog. It tears people apart who wish to be taken seriously, but I could not help myself. There were many complaints and finally a man in a brown suit came and looked at me. He was very important and not used to being laughed at, but he had dandruff on his collar, and there was a spot of his breakfast egg on his lapel. You should have seen him – so puffed up and proud of himself. I couldn't help but laugh and that made people see him as I did, and so they laughed too. All of a sudden everyone realised that for all his status in official matters, he was a man who lived alone and loveless. Anyone he lived with would have told him in a friendly fashion about those little imperfections. It was clear to all of them that he was hopelessly lonely and had no one to love him, that he had no life other than in his official capacity as an inspector. Pity for him made me laugh. I laughed and laughed and the audience was ravaged by it. The ringmaster said it was the final straw and so they exiled me from the circus and brought me here.'

'I heard you laughing,' 'Jack said. He wanted to say something about the quality of that terrible laughter, but he did not know how to begin. So he said, 'I've never heard anyone laugh like you do.'

'Mine is pure laughter, I'm afraid. Very potent. But I laugh at myself most often,' the beast murmured.

'Why are you *here*, I meant before,' Jack explained

apologetically. 'In the greylands?'

'Ahh! I misunderstood you. But *greylands*, eh? Well, naming is what happens to everything in the end. Names and cages, they are the same thing. First I was named, and that shaped me as I am, but then I was caged and this taught me pain, and in my pain I learned wisdom. I am here because laughter is a reflection of life too, do you see? Like a mirror.'

Jack had never thought of laughter that way, though it was true that sometimes when you started to laugh it made other people do the same thing. Like yawning. But laughter here seemed to mean something quite different to what it meant in his world, maybe simply because in reflections everything was back to front. Laughter had got back to front as well, for in the greylands it seemed to have more to do with sorrow than with happiness.

'You do not look well,' the beast observed. 'Perhaps you should sit and rest awhile.'

'I don't know how I could be so tired in a dream but I am,' Jack sighed.

'0, dreams can be far more tiring than life,' the beast said.

'This one sure is. It's the strangest dream I've ever had. I don't know where it began and I can't seem to wake from it,' Jack said.

The beast seemed to shake its head. 'So. You think you are inside a dream? Well, why not after all? I suppose you could call this grey land a dream of sorts. In any case it does not matter whether this is a dream or a real place. You are here, whichever it is.'

'It matters to me,' Jack said. 'If this was real, I could get back home through the mirror in that tent. But because it's a dream I can't escape.'

'Why not?' asked the laughing beast. 'Perhaps the way out of a dream is also through the mirror.'

'I just tried the mirror in that tent and I'm still here.'

The beast gave a melancholy chuckle. 'If at first you don't succeed, try again.'

Jack realised it was trying to cheer him up. He was not afraid of the beast at all and, to prove it, he came right up to the bars and curled his fingers around them. Looking into its sad, rather beautiful eyes, he thought about opening the cage.

'You must not let me out,' it warned him gently, as if it had read his mind. 'If you release me now that I know my nature, I could not help but unmake the enchantment of the mirrors. You see, they are tame now and they show only what people want and need to see in them. The wildness of them is bound up in my form, though I did not know it for a long time. If I were uncaged, I could not help but tear at the enchantment until I was unnamed. Then I would fly into all of the mirrors and windows and into shining footpaths after rain. All reflections would become wild and, they would be absolutely, utterly truthful. Everything would be seen for what it truly was. My laughter would greet every lie and every pretense. It would rumble like a volcano under the smooth surface of everything. You can imagine the chaos it would cause here, for those who dwell in the greylands do so because the mirrors are tamed. If I were free, people would come to be afraid of them. They would cease to believe in their reflections and eventually they would no longer believe in themselves. No, laughter must remain caged.'

'It's not caged where I come from,' Jack said.

The laughing beast smiled, baring fearsome white teeth. 'Are you sure of that? It may not be caged as here in the greylands, but there is very little completely wild laughter anywhere. *Children's* laughter, perhaps, for they have not learned to fear their faces in the mirror any more than they fear the truths of laughter and mirrors.'

'My mother said mirrors lie,' Jack said slowly. 'She was frightened of looking in them.'

'Many truths which are not believed are called lies,' the laughing beast said. 'But mirrors do not lie unless they have been enchanted to do so. Ordinary mirrors merely reflect what is revealed to them. *People* lie and mirrors reflect the lie as easily as if it were a truth. If your mother feared the mirrors in your land, she feared herself.'

Jack suddenly had an idea.

What if the mirror in the tent had failed to let him through because it was tame? Then his excitement ebbed, for Alice had said he could have gone back through the greylands bathroom mirror, and that must have been tame as well.

The beast was watching him intently. 'What is the matter?'

Jack shrugged. 'I just thought for a second that maybe I couldn't get through the mirror in the tent because it was tame. But maybe it is really just an ordinary mirror.'

'All mirrors in the greylands are enchanted to offer a way that is needed and wanted by those who gaze into them. A mirror would only refuse to let you pass if it saw that you did not really want to go back.'

'But I *do* want to go back!' Jack cried.

'Perhaps the mirror sees in you some fear of going back that you have hidden even from yourself.'

'There's nothing,' Jack insisted.

The beast gave him a long look. 'It need not be the fear of going back so much as the fear that going back will force you to see something that you do not want to see. The mirror would recognise that fear, if it existed even unknown to yourself, and seek to protect you from it.' The beast paused. 'I could help you, if you wish.'

'How?'

'Look to the mirror again and I will laugh. Face my laughter and yourself boldly and the mirror's enchantment will weaken enough to let you pass through.'

Jack felt excitement blur along his nerves, but it was also mingled with the anxiety that it might not work.

'I shall miss you if you succeed for few come here and even fewer would dare to speak with me,' the beast confessed sadly. 'I am not so bad, as you now see. And I know that I must remain caged for the protection of the wounded that seek refuge in the greylands, but it causes me pain when they talk about the dreadful power of my laughter and shun me utterly. But I can't help laughing. It just bursts out of me. But it doesn't mean I am *happy*. Happiness is the least reason for laughing.' It sighed heavily.

Pitying it, Jack wanted to say he would come back and visit the beast, but he did not want to make a promise that he might not be able to keep.

Again the laughing beast might have read his mind for it said, 'If you cannot come back to see me once you leave, you might see if you can find a way to send me a gift to remember you by. Something bright from your world. Things hold their colour for a while here when they are newly arrived.'

'I'll try,' Jack promised, as he bade it farewell.

His heart beat swiftly as he entered the tent again and faced the old mirror. The light was dim inside the thick canvas layers of the tent, and at first the laughter of the beast was muffled. But it grew louder and it seemed to Jack that his reflection gained colour as the beast's laughter gathered momentum.

It fluttered outside the tent like birds seeking entry. The tent shook and swayed under the force of it.

Jack wondered how long he could stand it. It reminded him of his mother's death and of Ellen crying in his arms. It reminded him of people saying they were sorry, sorry, so sorry.

It reminded him of seeing his father weep at the funeral.

'Mirror, Mirror, bring me home,' Jack chanted aloud.

The beast's laughter was louder now, as it if were seeping inside the tent. It flowed around him, lapped at him like a sea. He saw his father's face awash with tears. Then there were no tears and this was worse. His face was so dreadfully pale and his eyes were lifeless as stones. There was no warmth or brightness in them. No life. Better not to see him like that. Better never to see him again.

The laughter of the beast sobbed in the air that he breathed and Jack felt it enter him.

'Better never to return than to face such emptiness,' said the boy in the mirror.

Jack gasped as the knife of truth slid deeply into him. For it was true. He did not want to look at what his father had become and if he stayed here, he would not have to see it ever again. Was that what the enchanted mirror had seen? But as the beast's laughter simmered in his blood, Jack knew that it was only part of the truth. If it had been the only truth, he would not be here now, struggling to get home. There was another part of him that wanted to go back.

Still the mirror did not move, but Jack was no longer concentrating on it. The eyes in his reflection held him as he tried to figure out how he had become trapped here when only part of him wanted to stay. It must be that the part of him that wanted to stay was stronger than the part wanting to go back.

Jack could feel sweat running down his chest and the laughter carried him so deeply he felt he must drown, but he did not let go of the thread of his thoughts. He struggled to find what part of him wanted to return.

It was because of Ellen, of course. He could hardly leave her all alone to look after their father. Yet it was not duty alone. Something stronger drove him. Something hidden under duty.

A vision came to Jack of his sister sound asleep in her bed cuddling Mr Foo and something flared brightly in him.

Then he knew!

It was not duty that had made him open himself to the harrowing laughter of the beast, but love for Ellen.

Yet there was something even under that. It was not only love for Ellen that drew him back but also love for his father. He had to go back and he wanted

to go back because they belonged together. He and
Ellen and their father.

All for one and one for all. Always. All ways . . .

Jack felt his desire to return swell. In the mirror,
his eyes blazed blue, and his image started to ripple.
He laughed in triumph and reached out.

Chapter 7

'You have to be like a bird,' Mr Martin said. 'You have to swoop on the ball and carry it away.' He made a swooping motion to show them how he wanted them to do it.

'What sort of bird is that, sir?' asked Mario. 'There are lots of birds. I mean, the emu, but it can't fly. Then there's pigeons and cuckoos and the dodo.'

Jack had to look down at the pockmarked desk to stop from laughing. Mario was an expert at stalling and it was raining outside.

'That's enough, Mario,' Mr Martin said firmly. He was new at the school and you could see he was determined not to let them get on top of him.

'But I was just wondering, sir. I mean, there's birds and birds.' Mario sounded serious and a bit wounded, and though Jack couldn't look at him, he knew his friend would have that puzzled earnest look on his face that drove teachers crazy, because he was being cheeky but he wasn't *acting* cheeky, so they couldn't be sure if he wasn't just a bit stupid. He only tried it on new teachers because all of the others knew how smart he was.

'Mario, forget about birds, okay. It was just an example but maybe it wasn't a great example.' Mr Martin sounded tired.

'That's true, sir, because birds don't have hands, anyway, so how would they pick the ball up?'

Jack began to feel his brains pressing against his scalp with the effort of holding in laughter. Any minute and his ears would shoot off the side of his head. If he laughed now he would get detention for sure.

'Mario, enough with the birds, okay?' Mr Martin was saying. 'Think of a monkey, instead, pouncing on the ball and swinging away with it. My point is that you have to be quicker.'

'1 saw a monkey playing golf on television once,' Mario said in an eager-beaver voice.

It was too much. Jack started to splutter.

Mario pounded his back enthusiastically. 'Sorry, sir, it's all the talk of birds and monkeys. Jack's allergic to fur and feathers, you see.'

A burst of laughter got tangled up with Jack's breathing and a high-pitched wheezing sound came out of him.

'This has happened before?' Mr Martin asked, sounding worried. Jack could tell from the pause that Mario was figuring the angles.

'It's never happened at school before,' he said,

carefully not saying it had never happened anywhere else either. 'He just needs to lie down for a bit.'

'Okay, Mario. Help him to the change room and you can both finish up. You make sure he gets home. The rest of you get out there on the field and we're going to do some laps for the last ten minutes.'

The others groaned as Mario helped Jack to his feet. Jack didn't dare look into Mr Martin's face. They barely made it to the change room before collapsing into hysterics.

'Did you see how he looked?' Mario gasped. 'He really thinks you can get an allergic reaction from talking about things. Okay!' He mimicked Mr Martin.

'He'll probably check,' Jack said, dabbing at his eyes.

'So what? The school doesn't know everything.'

'What if they call my dad?'

Mario became immediately serious, almost as if he knew what Jack's father was like now. 'You answer the phone and tell them you made it up and that you told me as a joke. Say you didn't know I'd blurt it out like that and you didn't say anything because you didn't want to make me look bad.'

'So why was I coughing?'

'You had just swallowed a fly. Eating insects could run in the family,' Mario said with a leer. 'I have to pee,' he added, and went into the toilets.

Jack lay along the bench and closed his eyes.

Outside he could hear some guys talking and somewhere someone was practising the piano. He realised he felt happier than he had in a long time. He knew why, of course. It was not Mario's antics so much as his triumphant return from the greylands. He wished he could tell Mario what had happened. But he could just imagine how the conversation would go.

'So, what you're saying is the first time you came out of this grey world you fell off a building and landed on the end of Ellen's bed, and the second time, you landed on the couch.'

'The second time was a dream,' Jack would cut in, though the fact that his schoolbag had mysteriously vanished made him less sure of that.

'Ohhh. I see,' Mario would say sarcastically. 'You were taking a stroll in a grey world and you fell asleep and dreamed you were back home reading a story to Ellen. Then you went to sleep in the dream and woke up in grey world again?'

'The greylands,' Jack would say flatly, seeing how it sounded.

'Whatever. You don't think it's a bit of a lucky coincidence you would escape this place through a random mirror and somehow find its reflection matching your bedroom?'

'It *didn't* match my bedroom. I think the laughing beast made it bring me to my own bedroom.'

About now, Mario would cut the sarcasm and start thinking Jack was mentally disturbed. 'How do you know you didn't dream this escape? Dreams can seem pretty real.'

'I didn't wake up in my bed. I was just on it. I still had all my clothes on.'

'So what? I always sleep with my gear on so I don't have to waste time getting dressed in the morning.'

'Well, I don't. Normal people don't sleep with their clothes on,' Jack would snap back.

'I don't think a guy who goes jumping through mirrors into other worlds is any authority on normality,' Mario would wisecrack. 'Anyway are you saying you've never slept with your clothes on?'

'No! Well, a couple of times. But not this time.'

'You told me you dreamed this place up?'

'I know, because I *thought* it was a dream.'

'So how come you're suddenly so sure it's *not* a dream?'

There was no answer to that. After all, whoever heard of a real place you entered through a mirror and where there was no colour and a beast laughed in sorrow? It sounded as unreal as something out of a book, though one of Jack's English teachers once said that a lot of make-believe stuff in books wasn't exactly unreal, because you weren't supposed to see it as real in the first place. You were supposed to see it as a symbol of something else. Wings on a girl might be a symbol for the fact that she had really high-flying dreams, or maybe a man might be made into an ogre to show how cruel and mean he was. In a way, symbols showed the insides of things.

Jack started to drift off, so he got up and went to the drink fountain. Lapping at the bubble of water that erupted, he thought about his father. If only he could help him, but what could he do? He was just a kid. It wasn't even as if he had someone to go to. His dad didn't have any brothers or sisters and his own mother and father were long gone. Even his mother's father was dead, and her mother had Alzheimer's. He could call her companion, but she didn't like Jack's father because she was afraid he would try to get the old woman to change her will.

Jack crossed to the stainless-steel hand basin and looked into the spotty mirror above it. He looked the same, though he kept feeling that something of his strange adventures must show in his face.

'I don't want to interrupt you admiring yourself,' Mario said, having come out of the toilet unnoticed. 'But I gotta go.'

'Go where? School's not even officially over yet.'

'I'm going to my mum's place this weekend.' Mario pulled on his raincoat. 'If I get there early I get to pick the videos. You wouldn't believe what she picks on her own. She got *Bambi* last time. Come on, you can walk me to the city bus stop.'

After Mario had gone off on his bus, Jack walked home. He was still grinning at Mario's parting insults, and found himself wishing Mario had invited him away for the weekend, but why should he when

Jack never asked him over anymore? Jack decided suddenly that he *would* ask if Mario could come to dinner on Sunday night the way he'd used to. Maybe he could break the deadly silence in the house.

'No,' his father said.

Jack did not know how to argue against such an absolute no. It was as if his father had thumped a piece of stone down on the table.

'Please, Daddy,' Ellen said eagerly. 'I like Mario.'

He did not answer. He did not even look at Ellen, who blinked hard and bit her lip. Jack's anger rose up and engulfed his elation. Couldn't their father at least pretend to be interested in what his daughter was saying? He had lost a wife, but so had Ellen lost a mother. She was just a little girl but she hadn't just given up and let herself die inside. Nor had he, Jack thought, though remembering how hard it had been to leave the greylands, he understood that he had almost done so.

In anger and defiance he started to sing a stupid song Mario sometimes sang about worms. It was hard to sing in that thick, forbidding silence, but he did and, after her first startled look, Ellen laughed and clapped her hands in delight.

Jack saw his father shiver as if the sound of it stung him. 'That's enough,' he said flatly.

He got up and began to collect the plates, even though Jack wasn't completely finished. Going to the sink, he stumbled over the phone cord but caught himself on the edge of the bench. Then he just stood there looking down at the dirty plates he was holding.

'Go and brush your teeth. It's time for bed,' he whispered at last.

Jack got up and took Ellen's hand.

'Goodnight, Daddy,' she called. Then, 'Oww! Jack, you're hurting my hand holding it so tight.'

'Sorry,' he muttered.

Lying in his bed later, Jack tried to recall how happy he had been in the greylands when the mirror rippled and he had seen he would be able to get home. He could *remember* feeling glad, but he could not recapture it. He felt as if he had brought home a jug of molten gold to his father, and had seen it poured onto the ground. He had felt angry in the kitchen over the way their father acted towards Ellen, but now he could only feel pity for him, and a kind of helpless despair for them all. It seemed to him that some of the dull flatness of the greylands had leaked inside him.

For some reason, he thought of Alice.

She had been so pretty despite her lack of colour, but liking her wasn't the same liking he felt for the red-haired girl who sometimes caught the bus with him. What he felt for Alice was closer to what he felt about Ellen. Especially when she had seemed vulnerable and frightened. He had wanted to protect her and stop her being so scared. But it was also because she had taken his hand in the dark when *he* was scared. And even with her sudden fits of temper, her coldness and her paranoia over the bundle she carried, Alice had a strange glamour. He wished he had been able to learn more about her.

There were so many unanswered questions swarming around in his head about the greylands. For instance how had Alice got there in the first place, and what was in her mysterious bundle and why did the wolvers want to destroy it? And why had *he* been drawn there, and how? It couldn't just be that he had touched the mirror, or people would be falling through into the greylands all the time. Alice said you had to be wounded, but there had been nothing wrong with him. He wished he had asked the laughing beast about it. It had seemed so wise and kind. Maybe it would even have been able to figure out a way for Jack to save his father.

Jack drifted asleep and dreamed he was walking along the beach with his mother. They passed the lifesaver flags and she gave them a brooding look.

'Saving someone is a serious business,' she said. 'Some people believe you are responsible for the life you save. And maybe people don't always want to be saved.' Jack glanced up at his mother, but she did not look at him. 'Think how you would feel if you were Rapunzel locked up in that tower for years and years with only the old witch visiting you and bringing you food every few days,' she said.

'I would be lonely and unhappy,' Jack said, though he didn't understand what this had to do with rescuing people.

'No,' his mother said. 'Because you wouldn't know what it was like to be anything but alone. It would seem normal to you. You would weave, and every now and then the witch would cut off some of your hair to sell. That would be your life.'

'But Rapunzel could see out of the tower,' he had argued. 'She would see other people and animals and flowers and she would wish to be free.'

His mother shook her head. 'No. You see the witch would have told her everything she saw from the window was poisonous or dangerous or frightening and Rapunzel would have no reason to doubt her. She would be glad to be safe. She would feel how lucky she was.'

'She was happy?' Jack said doubtfully.

'She was. Then the prince came to rescue her. He would call to her to throw down her braids and he would convince her to come down from the tower with him. He would tell her he loved her and she would go because she was accustomed to being obedient and because she was dazzled by the prince.'

'She would be scared though,' Jack said.

'She would, but she would not want the prince to know. Everything would be strange to her. She would know nothing about how to behave and people would stare at her and whisper about her. She would keep her unhappiness locked up inside her, but slowly she would learn that her life had been wrong in the eyes of the world. She would be ashamed of it and of her contentment. She would go mad and in the end she would return to the tower so they would not have to see her madness.'

'They should have left her,' Jack said, seeing this was the point of the story, but he felt unsettled at the thought of the golden-haired princess spending her whole life in a tower, and knowing nothing of the world. Surely the prince would have loved her enough to see how unhappy she was?

His mother let go of his hand and turned suddenly to the sea. Her lips were painted red and her dark hair flew back in the wind like a flag. She dropped her towel and plunged into the waves. Jack followed and swam with her for a bit but the sea was rough and the undertow pulled at him hungrily so he came in to shore. He spread his towel on the sand and sat watching his mother swimming. The sun was so warm that after a moment he stretched out and closed his eyes. The sea roared in his ears, and he felt as if he was still swimming. He seemed to be floating back and back.

'Help!' his mother cried. Suddenly she sounded very far away.

Jack opened his eyes in fright and sat up quickly.

He was lying on a bench in a mirror image of the school change room. Everything was turned around the other way, and instead of dirty green walls, the change room had grey walls and lacked the unmistakable sweaty sock smell of the real change room. This room smelled like no one had been in it for a hundred years.

Standing up he went outside. Even though he knew better, he half expected to find himself on the oval, but of course the reflection was only of the inside of the school change rooms. Outside he found himself looking out over a flat plain stretching out of sight, broken only by a few boulders and scrubby trees. He turned and saw that the building he had come from looked nothing like the school change rooms. It was a foreign-looking white stone building with a flat roof and small, high, square windows. There were a lot of other buildings behind it that looked the same. The whole scene reminded him of a calendar photograph of buildings baking in the sun on a Greek island.

Only there was no sun here. There was just grey brightness.

'Help!'

Jack swung around startled. The faint cry had seemed to come from behind him, but, scanning the plain, he couldn't see anyone. Maybe it had been a bird, though he had not seen any animals or birds or even insects here except the cats. He hadn't seen anyone other than Alice and the laughing beast, but they had both spoken of others. The beast had even talked of a circus audience.

'Help!'

Jack recognised Alice's voice.

He looked around and finally he spotted her lying some distance, away in a shallow depression. She was half hidden by a pile of boulders, so it was no wonder he hadn't seen her. When he got to her, he found she was dressed in the same plain cotton tunic, sandals and cloak as before, but her cloak was thrown aside. To his amazement he saw that she really did have wings. Until that moment he had thought she'd lied. They were like a bird's wings, except that the feathers were much bigger and longer and shaded white blending down to pearl grey.

She moaned and Jack knelt beside her. 'What's wrong?' He could see she was in pain, but he had learned in first-aid classes not to do anything until he had some idea of the injuries involved.

'It's my wings,' Alice gasped. 'They're trapped. I fell and I can't reach to get myself free.' Her face screwed up the way you do when you're trying not to cry. 'Can you get me out?'

Jack looked more closely and found that some of the feathers at the bottom of the wing were jammed between the boulders. One long feather lay on the ground nearby with a drop of darkness at its base.

Blood was black in the greylands.

'Hurry up!' Alice groaned.

Jack began to pull at one of the boulders. The effort of shifting it even the smallest bit made him grunt, but abruptly the wing tip was free. 'There,' he said, smoothing the feathers. One was bent rather badly. As he helped Alice to her feet, he noticed that her clothes had holes in the back so that the wings could poke out. 'What happened?' he asked.

'The wolvers were chasing me and I fell,' she answered quickly, dismissively.

'How come they didn't take the bundle?' Jack asked.

'You think I made it up?' she demanded sharply.

Jack said nothing.

'All right,' she admitted sullenly. 'It wasn't the wolvers. I was climbing up on the rocks. I was trying to see the grey tower and I fell.'

'Why?' Jack still had the feeling she was not telling the whole truth.

'I have to go there.' She pulled the cloak around her shoulders. Jack wondered why she kept her wings covered all the time.

'Why don't you just fly there?'

Alice pretended not to have heard. Or maybe she *didn't* hear him. Either way, Jack had the feeling she might have been trying to fly when she fell and got her wing stuck. She had said that having wings was not all that great and maybe this was because she hadn't figured out how to use them. Or, possibly, the bundle hampered her.

As if she had heard, his thought, she began examining it again. Jack bent down to pick up the feather that had come out of her wings. It felt silky and was twice as long as his hand. The tip shimmered slightly. He slipped it carefully inside his coat pocket.

'You have been lucky the wolvers haven't caught you,' Alice said, tucking the bundle under her arm, and Jack understood that she didn't realise he had been back home since they had last parted.

'I went back through the mirror,' he said. 'The laughing beast helped me.'

Alice's eyes widened and for a moment he thought she would question him about the beast and ask why he had returned, but she only said they had better go quickly then because the wolvers would have been alerted by his crossing and must already be on their way.

She hastened past the building, which, inside, was the reflection of the school change room, and plunged into the maze of narrow dirt streets running between the square white buildings.

'You decided to come back to stay?' she demanded after they had been walking for a bit.

Jack shook his head. 'I didn't decide anything. I don't even remember coming through a mirror, though I suppose I must have done, since I am here.

Maybe wanting to know more about this place drew me back.'

Alice said with sharp reproof, 'Wanting does not belong here. Those who come to dwell in the greylands are seeking the end of wanting. But if they cannot stop wanting even here, the wolvers deal with them.'

'The wolvers don't go after everyone?'

'Only those who cannot escape wanting on their own. They must have wings to kill their wanting.'

'But you want to go to the grey tower and you have wings,' Jack said.

Instead of answering, Alice stroked her bundle and said dreamily, 'Once upon a time a woman came to a faraway land. She was very tired when she arrived but she had to go to a banquet. Do you know that story? I should like to hear it again.'

The words were familiar, but Jack couldn't re-member where he had heard them before. Alice had started to walk more quickly and as before he was finding it hard to keep up. 'Wait for me,' he called.

She looked back and said, 'I must hurry. I must get to the tower as soon as I can. It will be difficult and dangerous to avoid the wolvers.'

'Maybe I could help,' Jack said. 'I could be a decoy.'

'You are too slow. They would kill you for your effort,' Alice said bluntly.

'Well, why don't you just leave the bundle hidden somewhere while you go to the tower?' He didn't make the mistake of suggesting he take care of it.

'I have to bring it to the tower,' Alice said, and Jack saw a deep sadness in her eyes that made him shiver inside.

'Who lives in the grey tower?' he asked.

'You are funny,' Alice said quite kindly. 'No one does.'

'Somebody must.'

'Everything comes to the grey tower in the end, but nothing lives there.'

'Who gives out the wings then?'

'I told you, they grow after you go there and then you are part of the greylands for ever. You join the soft and the silent and the painless.'

'Why are *you* going there?' Jack asked. 'You already belong. You have wings.'

Alice's eyes fell to the bundle she carried. But she only said, 'People from the other side of the mirror always want to know who and where and why and what is the name. They have to know everything. They are always gnawing at things and at one another.'

'It's good to want to know things,' Jack said defensively.

'It is? What happens when there is no answer?' she sneered. 'Wanting-to-know is always biting at you. Biting and itching. You want too much. Go back to your own world. You don't belong here.'

She turned around the next corner and, following, Jack found himself looking down a steep city street lined with tall shining skyscrapers, all reflecting one another and bits of the grey sky. Disoriented because he had not seen any skyscrapers above the buildings they had been passing through, he looked back. He could only see a little of the street they had just come from, which sort of merged and blurred at the edges. It was as if a mist was closing over behind him.

Jack turned back to ask Alice a question, but the street of skyscrapers was quite deserted. Alice had disappeared.

The Middle

'What do you think of it so far?' Jack asked.

'I like it but . . . it's not about Mama dying and Daddy's heart being lost,' Ellen said.

'What happened after Mama died is not something you can tell by just talking about real things. It's an inside story.'

'Like symbols?' Ellen asked.

Jack nodded. 'It's real things turned inside out so you can see what the inside is like. Because just telling what happened wouldn't show the inside stuff. It wouldn't tell how I finally figured out about Mama being sick. It wouldn't show how Dad got worse and worse after she died, and it wouldn't explain how we felt.'

'Mama was muddled up like in your story. She saw real things, but sometimes she saw things that weren't real either,' Ellen said gravely.

'Mama saw things inside herself but she didn't know they were from inside her. She thought they were real,' Jack said.

Ellen nodded. 'I knew Mama was sick.'

'I know you did. But I didn't.'

'Daddy should have told you.'

'I think he's figured that out, now. But he didn't tell us because he couldn't bear to talk about what was happening to her. He made it a secret and after she died, he got lost in the secret.'

'What are the wolvers? Are they werewolfs?'

'Werewolves,' Jack corrected. 'But they're not wolves or werewolves. They're *symbols* of what you feel when you think about wolves.'

'I feel scared. I think about being crunched up in their teeth!'

'That's what wolvers are: the fear of being crunched up. They're symbols of fear. Alice thinks they sniff out people, who want too much, but fear is what they smell. Fear always chases after its own tail. They chase Jack because he is scared for his dad and they smell it.'

Ellen pondered that for a moment. 'I like the laughing beast. I'm not scared of *him*. He's a symbol too, right?'

'Right. When people are scared of themselves, they are afraid of laughter most of all because it's like a mirror that reflects their fear. That's why the wolvers are scared of him.'

Ellen said, 'Alice is scared of the laughing beast because she's scared of herself?' Jack said nothing. 'I don't like her,' Ellen added.

'Alice? Why not?'

'She never tells him anything and she keeps thinking he's trying to steal from her and then going off and leaving him. I don't know why he likes her. She didn't even say thank you when he helped with her wings.' Ellen frowned. 'I mean, when *you* helped her.'

'Say he, it's easier. The Jack in the story isn't really me, anyway. It's partly me and partly made up. It's the inside me that went to the greylands.'

They were silent for a moment.

'What is he going to do with the feather?'

'I don't know yet.'

'I think he should give the feather to the poor laughing beast,' Ellen said. 'What's the shining thing in the bundle?' She tapped the page. 'Why do the wolvers want to destroy it?'

'Because it's the opposite of them. But I'm not telling you what it is. Figuring it out is part of the story.'

'Give me a clue,' Ellen demanded.

'It's one of the inside things,' Jack said. 'It's something real inside something I made up. It's a symbol.'

'Why is Alice taking it to the tower?'

'You have to work that out yourself.'

'Why do you have to make it hard?' Ellen grumbled.

'Because it was hard for me to figure it out,' Jack said. 'That's the truth and why should you get it easier than me? Now shut up and let me write. Don't interrupt any more until I've finished.'

Jack stood in the middle of the street, dwarfed by the soaring skyscrapers. They were like a square shining forest of glass and he felt very alone and also oddly disappointed. On the other side of the mirror he remembered the greylands as exciting and exotic, but now that he was here, he found it hard to feel anything much.

Seeing Alice really had wings had thrilled him, but she never flew and she always kept them covered so they might just as well have been a hump on her back for all the joy she had of them. Everything was so numb and flat and drab, even feelings. Especially feelings. But he supposed that was how the wounded people here liked it. Like hospitals always being restfully dull and undemanding. But it would be terrible never to smell anything again, or see any colour. Jack's eyes were beginning to ache at the softness of everything.

He wished Alice had at least said goodbye. He would have liked to go to the grey tower with her, though she was right about him not being capable of outrunning the wolvers. But maybe he could have gone some of the way, and she could have told him how to find his way back to the laughing beast.

He had told her the truth when he said he didn't know why he had returned to the greylands, or even how. But since he was there, he might as well visit the laughing beast and ask about helping his father. Besides that, he might need its help to get home again. Maybe he could have gone back to the change rooms and used the mirror there, but the grey mistiness behind and in front of him in the distance gave him the uneasy feeling that the greylands dissolved around the edges of wherever you were standing. After all, it wasn't exactly real, was it? It was just a reflection of real places. And the lack of colour gave everything a dreamy quality that made you think it hadn't the same solidity as the real world.

Jack noticed a small street leading off from the main artery. At the corner he stopped to look down it but there was no sign of Alice. Continuing along the main street, he went back to pondering why she would suddenly want to take the bundle to the grey tower when it sounded as if it would be swarming with wolvers. Hadn't she been running and hiding from them? And what was in the grey tower anyway, other than something that planted wings? In a book there would be a powerful wizard, but Alice had said that no one lived there.

His dream of being at the beach with his mother,

and her belief that the princess ought to have been left in the tower, made him wonder if the tower would be a safe place once you got inside it, despite being surrounded by wolvers. Maybe Alice just wanted finally to be safe. She had seemed really bothered when he said she was putting her bundle in danger in the wildness. It was even possible that was why she had decided to go to the tower.

Tired of speculating, Jack concentrated on walking. His sneakered footsteps echoed with a flat little thump, and he thought how odd it was to be in a silent, empty city. Even in the middle of the night in a real city there would be people – a drunk or a policeman or a fat taxi driver asleep behind the wheel. This city was not only empty; it felt as if no one had ever lived here. It didn't smell like a real city and it didn't sound like a real city.

In fact, it didn't even act like a proper city

The windows of the shops he was passing were tinted dark and shiny, so that you couldn't see what was inside, and there were no signs or billboards anywhere, and no neon lights flashing. Most of all, there were no other people. Jack's reflection looked very small and lonely.

He tried a door in one of the buildings, but it was locked. Maybe it was not even a real door, be thought. Everything in the greylands might be like a set on a stage: it looked real, but it was a trick. The more he thought about that, the more likely it seemed.

Mirrors lie, his mother had said.

Pretending is a kind of lying, his father had said. A city that pretended to be a city was a lie then. A trick.

You had to trick the truth out of the mirror, his mother had said.

On impulse, Jack stopped and turned to look into a window, but his reflection only stared palely back at him. He noticed that once again his eyes were dark grey. He willed the reflection to let him through, but the glass remained still. He wasn't surprised.

He heard a noise, and looked over his shoulder, but the street was still utterly deserted. The noise came from rain that had begun to fall. Big drops that splashed onto the grey pavement and the black road, and spotted the windows.

Jack sat down on a sill, deciding to wait under its awning until it stopped. He glanced back at the glass and was astounded to see reflected behind him a man wearing an overcoat and carrying a briefcase. He had just come out of a door.

'Hey!' Jack cried, leaping to his feet.

There was no one in the street. Jack looked back at the window in bewilderment and there was the man in the raincoat looking around and scratching his head under his hat.

Jack looked back at the street, and it was empty. Then he understood. The man was nothing more than a reflection. Jack watched him walked to the edge of the glass, shaking his head, and vanish.

Jack closed his mouth, trying to understand. Had the man walked past a window in the real world, and shown for a second here in the greylands? In that brief moment, had he heard Jack shout? And why hadn't the man seen *him?*

More questions, Jack thought. The greylands seemed to contain only mysteries and questions, like holding two mirrors facing one another, so that they simply reflected themselves infinitely. You could never get to the end of them.

'What are you doing?' Alice's voice rapped at him sharply.

Jack turned to find she was sheltering under an awning further down the street. He felt a wash of relief go through him as she beckoned impatiently. Afraid she might vanish again, he ran out into the rain and down to where she was standing in a doorway under another awning. He was startled to discover that the falling rain had not wet him.

Jack wondered if Alice had been waiting for him, or had simply been delayed by the rain. He said, 'I saw a man in the window back there. Just his reflection, just for a moment.'

Alice nodded. 'That happens sometimes. A lot of people almost come over for a little without realising it.'

'But he *heard* me,' Jack protested, feeling that Alice's explanation was too simple.

'Maybe he did. If *you* can come and go, I guess

your voice can. Mine can't, because of the wings.'

'I saw you in the mirror that first night,' Jack said.

'That's impossible. You imagined it.'

Jack thought crossly that she was a fine one to be talking about imaginary things. He decided to try asking her some of the questions buzzing around in his head while they were waiting for the rain to stop.

'Did you come from my side of the mirror, Alice?'

'Everyone starts off there,' she said absently, peering up at the sky.

'Did the wolvers catch you and take you to the tower?'

'There was no need. I was looking for the tower. All my life I dreamed of it. I wanted to climb it, but no one would let me. They said people who live in the world of smells and colour can't climb the grey tower. So one day, when no one was watching, I climbed it.'

'That's when they gave you the wings?'

'I had them all along inside me, waiting to grow. I have to go now,' Alice said nervously, her eyes flicking back and forth.

'Are you really going to the grey tower again?'

Alice didn't answer and it struck Jack that this was how she dealt with questions she did not like. She either heard them wrongly, or pretended not to hear them at all. He decided not to press her.

'The rain has stopped,' she said.

So it had. The street was already dry, and Jack

could not imagine why she had taken shelter from the rain. She must know it would not wet her. Somehow that had not surprised him very much. Probably fire wouldn't burn you either.

'Are you coming?' Alice asked. She did not wait for him to say yes or no, but set off down the street again. She seemed to have forgotten that she wanted to be alone and Jack hurried to keep up, not wanting her to remember.

'I'm going to the circus,' she said, looking at him. Her eyes glittered with excitement. 'I like the circus.'

'The *circus?*' Jack echoed, no less astonished than if she had said she was going to dig up a few graves at the local cemetery. Then he remembered that the laughing beast had spoken of a circus and he wondered if it was the same one. He was about to ask Alice when she stopped suddenly.

'Here it is.' She pointed down another street running away from the main road. Incredibly, although they were in the middle of a city, down the end of it was an enormous fenced field. From where they were standing most of it was cut off from their view by the edges of the skyscrapers, and the greyness stopped him from seeing the far side of the field, or what lay beyond, but right in the centre of it was an enormous striped tent with some smaller tents scattered around it.

Jack had the strangest feeling he had seen them before.

He followed Alice to the field gate. A swaying necklace of lights flickered above a sign, which read: Enter at Own Risk.

Jack didn't like the sound of that. 'I thought you were going to the grey tower,' he stalled. 'I thought you were in a hurry.'

'It doesn't matter which way you go,' she said absently, switching the bundle from one arm to the other.

That made so little sense, Jack simply followed her across the field to the big tent. Now he could see there were several caravans and cage trailers between the big top and the smaller tents. There were also a lot of trailer cages like the one that had held the laughing beast, though probably there were no animals in them just the same as there were no people.

'Where is the audience?' he asked, to see what Alice would say.

'Someone is always watching,' she murmured cryptically.

They had reached the big tent by now. There was no wind blowing but the tent sides were flapping wildly as if animated by some inner storms.

'Maybe I shouldn't come,' Jack said, mindful of the sign, but she had already slipped into the nearest tent.

Jack lingered outside unable to make up his mind whether to go in or not. He spotted someone moving between the caravans.

'Hey, you! Stop!' he cried.

A short, lean man in white trousers and a leather apron turned to face him, thick, black brows raised in enquiry. Despite the eyebrows, the man was bald. His head was so shiny it looked as if he'd polished it.

'You'd better be careful who you're shouting at in that rude way,' he said mildly.

Jack was so surprised to be spoken to normally that he didn't know what to say. The truth was he had half expected the man to vanish or make some crazy statement or just run away.

'Didn't you see the sign?' the man asked, coming over to him. 'It said: Enter at your own risk.'

'I saw it,' Jack stuttered. 'But my friend is here. She . . . she had something to do here. She's in there.' He pointed to the big top.

The man's brows tilted up into his bald head. 'She's one of the winged ones then?'

'You don't have wings,' Jack realised.

The man shook his head. 'Oh no. Them in the big top like to think everyone here has them or means to get them, but it's not true.'

'What about the wolvers? Don't they go after anyone without wings?'

'They only go after ones as need to be winged. They don't trouble the rest of us,' the man said comfortably.

'They keep chasing me,' Jack said, though more to himself than to the man. He wondered suddenly if he had only *imagined* they were chasing him, because hadn't he always been with Alice when they turned up. It was she who had told him they were after him, but maybe she was wrong.

'They chase the ones as needs wings,' the man repeated and gave him a narrow look. 'I wouldn't have picked you for one of that type, though you never know with people. If you are hanging around with one of the winged ones you can get like them in the end.' He shrugged meaningfully.

'Why do the winged people come to the circus?' Jack asked.

'Not all do. But there are a lot of them here because they can be sure of being seen. They hate being looked at, but they don't believe in themselves unless someone can see them. Being seen is believing, see? Not believing in yourself is a disease and in the end it sends you mad. Maybe that's why the wolvers are after you. They could smell that you don't believe in yourself. That's something the wings heal too, along with wanting and being afraid. But it's a drastic solution and there's no going back from it.'

'Do you . . . do you live here?'

'I am living here and I live here and don't ask why or how long, for it's no business of yours. But you're an accidental, aren't you,' the man said. 'You don't see too many of your kind around.'

'How do you know?' Jack asked nervously. 'Is it my eyes being coloured sometimes?'

The man laughed. 'Bless you, boy. Those of us who live in the greylands couldn't see colour if it was to hit us in the face. You'll find *you* can't see it any more after a while either. Truth is it's a great relief to leave the colours and all of that fuss and brightness on the other side.'

'Don't you miss the noise and the people and the smells? And the animals? How can you have a circus without animals?'

The man chuckled richly. 'As to the smells and the brightness, when I was on the other side they filled up my head so I could never think properly. And I don't miss people because I have my own voices in here.' He tapped his head. 'But animals? What makes you think that there are no animals here?'

Jack was confused by the amusement in the man's eyes. 'I didn't see any animals other than cats, not even elephants or horses.'

'Oh well, we don't have *them*,' the man said. 'But we have animals just the same. What would a circus be without animals? Didn't you see the cages?'

'I didn't see anything in them,' Jack said.

'That's because you're not staying here. And they know it just the same way I do.' The man tilted his head. 'You want to see them?'

Jack nodded eagerly. He didn't much like animals being kept in cages, but that was the only way you ever saw a lion or a tiger except on television.

The man led him over to the nearest cage. 'It's not

strictly allowed, you understand, you being an accidental, but maybe you'll come here of your choosing
soon, and I can stretch a point . . .'

The trailer cage was divided in two. Sitting in
one side, with its legs curled under it neatly, was a
small pony with a gleaming golden horn rising from
the centre of its forehead. It was asleep and snoring
slightly. On the other side was what looked like a lion
except when Jack looked at it properly; he saw it was
an enormous bird with a lion's head!

'These are not real animals!' he gasped.

The lion bird's golden eyes regarded him thought-
fully, and then it yawned widely, showing a mouth
and neck like a red tunnel.

Jack felt the blood rise in his face, because it came
to him the lion bird had understood his words. 'I
mean, there are none of them where I come from,'
he said apologetically.

'Of course not,' the man said, sounding almost
affronted. 'They can only come here because of the
enchantment of the mirrors.'

'How come its eyes and mouth are coloured? And
the horn?'

The man lifted his brows. 'Are they?'

Jack remembered then that people who lived in
the greylands could not see colour. He turned back
to the cage, but now it was empty.

'Ah well, they've gone,' the man said philosophi-
cally. 'What can you expect? They know you don't

belong here. That remark about them not being real gave you away completely. No one from here would say such a thing.'

Jack felt his cheeks grow warm again. 'I didn't mean to hurt their feelings,' he said humbly.

'Oh, they didn't go because their feelings were hurt,' the man assured him. 'They didn't *choose* to go. You made them disappear because you don't really believe in them. That's what happens to things that don't get believed in; sooner or later.'

Jack was aghast. 'You mean . . . they've gone for good?'

The man shrugged. 'I'm afraid so. They're delicate things, even here where they're mostly safe from disbelief. But perhaps someone will come along who will believe in them and they'll be back. Or something else will come. It could have been worse. Once a dragon came. We had a terrible time trying to stop it setting the customers on fire. That sort of thing is very bad for business and it was dreadful trying to get rid of it because it's awfully hard not to believe in something that is blowing flames at you! I told you all those who come to be part of the circus need to be seen, to believe in themselves. Seeing is believing and believing is seeing. That's what this circus is all about.'

'How did you know *I* wasn't from here?' Jack asked.

'First you can see colours in things. I'm told a bit

slips through here and there because not everyone comes here for always. But most of all, I can smell you. Nothing here smells, you see. Nothing that chooses to be here, I mean. Fee Fi Fo Fum, I smell your warm blood.' He tapped his nose and leaned close to Jack as if he meant to whisper something. Then he smiled, baring his teeth, and Jack saw with horror that they were all sharpened to points.

The man started to laugh loudly, and Jack staggered back.

'Run while you can, boy. Run back before the greylands drink your bright blood!'

Jack turned to run. He dashed between two smaller tents and came face to face with a mirror.

'1 want to go home!' he screamed, and he pictured Ellen as hard as he could, because thinking of her roused up a fierce longing to be home.

He almost wept with relief when the mirror began to ripple and buck, and he dived into it head first.

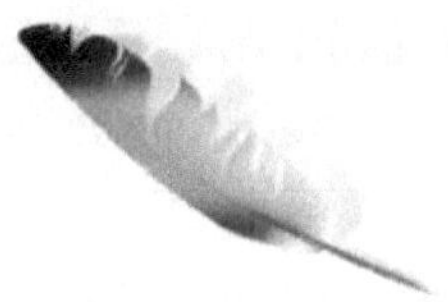

Chapter 9

Jack landed on his knees and palms, but the grazes were forgotten when he looked around.

He was in the fun park where his mother had died. Right in front of him was the mirror on the outside wall of the mirror maze. He backed away from it, chilled to the depths of his bones.

Now he understood why the greylands circus had felt so familiar. At least part of it was a reflection of the fun park, which had a big blue-and-white striped tent, surrounded by a number of smaller tents housing the sideshows. He had not been there since his mother died, but before that they had come all the time because she had liked it so much.

Jack stared at a chipped metal billboard announcing the Amazing Monster Man. This was a new attraction. The last time he had been here the billboard had advertised the Stupendous Snake Woman.

Jack turned away and looked around to get his bearings.

The park was way over the other side of town by the sea, and was closed because of it being out of season. Making his way along the narrow path between the dark booths and rides, Jack could hear the sea roaring on the other side of the fence, and he thought of the bald man in the greylands circus talking about the dragon that had come because someone had thought about it.

Maybe that was the reason there were dragons and all of that stuff in fairy tales. He could never figure out how somebody could think up things that weren't real. But maybe they *were* real, in a way. After all, dreams and stories were reflections of reality, so they must get themselves into the greylands too. It was kind of creepy to imagine something could come out of your imagination and be made real. What if you thought of a vampire or a werewolf?

His heart began to beat hard, and he tried not to think about vampires and stuff like that. He reached the perimeter of the park and was startled to see an enormous cat with tufted ears draped along the back of a roundabout pony. The cat blinked yellow eyes at him, but instead of feeling reassured by its presence, he felt cold and uneasy at the thought of it slinking back and forth between the real world and the greylands.

He had to climb over a fence to get out, and then he ran across the sand to the boardwalk. The sea was an inky murmur beside him as he made his way along it and then finally to the road.

It felt late, so Jack decided he had better spend his

pocket money and get a taxi home. His heart was still galloping even when he was safe and warm in the taxi. It cost almost all of his pocket money, but he was happy to spend it. His eyes devoured the driver's red neck above his pale-blue shirt. His ears strained to catch the sounds of the city: cars honking their horns, a man and woman on a corner shouting at one another, the screech of metal from a warehouse.

'Car twenty-nine to the corner of . . .' He heard a woman's voice from the taxi base. Then there was a burst of static mixed up with music from the radio. They passed a pizza shop and he sniffed up the smell of tomato and anchovies hungrily, his mouth watering. He could also smell the car fumes and some horrible chemical odour from the oil refinery on the edge of town, and even that smelled good to him.

He sighed and relaxed back into the seat. The real world was noisy and smelly but it was warm and bright and it was where he belonged.

He heard the sound of a woman giggling and that reminded him of the laughing beast and its mournful laughter. That was what happened to laughter when you caged it. It became unbearably sad. It was worse than crying. He was sorry he had not had a chance to see the beast again, but he was glad to be home.

He got the taxi to drop him on the corner of his street, and used a coin to call Mario from the phone box. Mario's father said he had gone to stay with his mother.

'Has my dad called?' Jack asked casually.

Mario's father said he hadn't, which meant his father wasn't checking around for him, and Jack had an alibi if he needed one. He could explain his late arrival by saying he had gone with Mario to the city bus stop.

When he got home the house was empty and silent and for a moment it seemed as if he had slipped back into the greylands. But in the kitchen, he found a note taped on the refrigerator door telling him that his father was working late. Jack was to pick Ellen up from next door when he came in.

'Next door!' he groaned. He would rather be told to pick her up from a crocodile-infested swamp than from the next-door neighbours.

'You're very late,' Mrs MacKenzie said, looking at him over her glasses.

Jack tried not to stare at her hair, which was a violent purple colour. Something must have gone wrong with her blue rinse. Or maybe his eyes were over sensitive because of being in the greylands.

'Choir practice,' he muttered.

'You're such a Good Boy,' Mrs MacKenzie gushed, and before he could avoid it, he found himself pressed into her squashy bosom. 'You're such a Help for your poor father.' Half suffocated, Jack bore it as long as he could, then he wriggled urgently and she let him go. Mrs MacKenzie's eyes had gone all watery and as usual she talked as though half the words were capitalised.

'I'm afraid he is still Very Depressed over your mother's death and who could wonder?' she said sympathetically. Her eyes were avid, though. Jack felt them on him like fingers, searching for a crevice to open him up.

'I've come for Ellen,' he told her stonily. What he wanted to say was: Curiosity killed the cat.

'Dear little girl.' Mrs MacKenzie dabbed at her eyes. 'I'm afraid she was Badly Affected by what happened. It's really not Natural for a child to be so neat and quiet and good. What happened appears to have retarded her, poor child. Such a Terrible Death for a little girl to understand. So macabre and so Odd, really.'

Mrs MacKenzie smiled, and Jack thought she ought to have sharpened teeth like the man in the greylands circus. She sounded concerned, but you could see she liked talking about hurtful things. If he came to her with a cut, he had the feeling she would push her fingers into the gash and smile in the same way.

'Ellen?' he gritted. He thought he saw disappointment flicker across the woman's face, but he might have imagined it.

'You didn't have choir practice. You told a lie,' Ellen accused, mercifully after the door had closed behind them. She was dressed in all-in-one pyjamas and a kimono of their mother's that had been cut down. Mr Foo was tucked firmly under her arm looking pop-eyed as ever.

'Old cow. Disgusting old moth-eaten cow,' Jack snarled, turning his back on the door and striding down the path. 'Lying doesn't count with people like Mrs MacKenzie.'

'Maggot,' Ellen said firmly, trotting along beside him.

Jack gave her a startled look. 'What?'

'I said maggot,' Ellen told him primly. 'It's a swear word.'

'No, it's not.' Jack grinned, his good humour restored.

'Yes it is, because a boy in school got a smack from his mother for saying it.'

Jack decided not to correct her. After all, it was a pretty good word to swear with.

'Maggot,' he agreed.

'Maggoty old Mrs MacKenzie,' Ellen said.

'You shouldn't call her that,' Jack chided. He was responsible for Ellen when their father was not home, and that meant being a good example. Her hand felt warm and soft and small in his, like a little animal. 'You shouldn't tell lies either unless it's really important to keep a secret.'

'Do *you* have a secret?' Ellen demanded, eyes wide.

Uh oh, Jack thought. That's what came of living with a budding genius. 'I do,' he admitted, still feeling ashamed about encouraging her to call Mrs MacKenzie a maggot.

'Tell me what it is!'

'But then it wouldn't be a secret, would it? Did you have anything to eat over there?'

They were in their own kitchen now, and food was usually the most effective way to divert her. Besides, Jack was starving, and not just for food: for the smells of food. Even boiled cabbage would be great. Or smoked fish. Well, maybe not smoked fish.

'I had mashed potato and beans,' Ellen said, frowning slightly. 'What is your secret? In the story, Kay and Gerda don't have any secrets because they love one another.'

It took Jack a minute to remember the story of the Snow Queen, but hadn't he just dreamed of reading it? It was harder and harder to remember what he had dreamed and what had really happened and he wondered if this was a side effect of his visits to the greylands.

'People who love one another don't have secrets,' Ellen concluded firmly.

'It's true you don't keep secrets from people you care about,' Jack said carefully. 'Though remember Mama had secrets and she made us not tell Dad?'

Ellen frowned and tilted her head at him. 'Mama

couldn't help it. The secrets got into her. They made her sick.'

Jack stared at his little sister. Sometimes he had the weird feeling she was older than him, and the things she said could be downright spooky. What on earth did she mean about secrets getting inside their mother? The phone rang.

'Hi, it's Mario. I'm at my mum's. My dad said you rang his place? What's up?'

'Nothing. Did you get to your mum's in time to pick a video?'

'Nah, so we've got *Ewok Adventure*.' He made a disgustingly realistic vomiting noise.

Jack laughed. 'Watch out! It might give you nightmares.'

'*You* give me nightmares!' Mario shouted. Jack heard a voice in the background call out something. 'Oops, gotta go. Say hi to Ellen and your dad!' He slammed the phone down the way he always did, and Jack hung up too, laughing.

'He said to say hi.'

'I like Mario,' Ellen said. 'I'm going to marry him when I grow up.'

Jack managed not to grin. This was new. 'Why?'

'He laughs a lot. Daddy used to laugh but he doesn't anymore because of the goblin's looking glass in his heart.'

'That's just a fairy story,' Jack said. 'Dad's just sad about Mama dying.'

'He was sad sometimes when she was alive,' Ellen said. 'Can I have a banana waffle?'

'You don't like bananas.'

'But Mario does,' Ellen said decidedly.

Jack was dreaming.

He was in the greylands circus with his mother. She had wings like Alice, and her face was pale. She had Alice's bundle under her arm.

'Let's climb the grey tower,' she said.

'Where is it?' Jack wondered.

'It's here. It's hidden but I know how to find it.'

'What's in that?' Jack pointed to the bundle.

His mother's eyes glittered. 'Do you want to see?'

Jack nodded, and watched mesmerised as she laid the bundle on a bench and started to unwrap it.

At last there was just one fold left.

'You must cover your eyes, or you will be blinded,' she whispered.

'What it is?' Jack asked.

His mother smiled, showing bright, sharp teeth. 'Curiosity killed the cat,' she whispered.

Jack woke, sweating and thinking a cat was in his room. He lay very still, but ran his eyes over everything. It was very dark and he had to steel himself to get out of bed and switch on the light.

Nothing happened. The bulb must have blown, he told himself, but he didn't really believe it. He thought of the cat at the fun park and wondered what would happen if a wolver somehow followed it into the real world.

He reached around the door for the hall light, but he couldn't feel the switch.

Then he heard a low, soft growl and nearly died of fright.

He stood frozen, but nothing leapt at him or growled again. After a long agonising moment, he wondered if maybe he had imagined it. He reached for the light again but still couldn't find the switch. Finally he had to force himself into the hallway. There was no switch and this was because he was standing in a strange hallway. But it was not completely strange. It was the same hall he had entered after coming into the greylands the first time.

Somehow he was back there again.

Which meant that maybe he hadn't imagined the growling after all. There might still be wolvers prowling around. But already the greylands were having an effect on him. Fear flickered in his chest, but it was like trying to light a wet candle. He simply couldn't be very frightened. It seemed that each time he came to the greylands, it was harder to feel things strongly.

Jack tiptoed down the ball, opened a glass door and peered into an old-fashioned living room with venetian blinds and grey carpet with big, darker grey flowers, hoping Alice would be somewhere around.

There must be some sort of link between them because they kept meeting.

There was a gas fire in the room and a mantelpiece over it laden with tiny statues and framed pictures. Even with the greylands numbness seeping through him, Jack was shocked to see that the photographs framed on the mantelpiece were of him and Ellen when they were younger. In one, their father was giving them a seesaw.

Jack was grinning and showing a gap where he had knocked a tooth out when he'd fallen off the front fence pretending to be the tightrope walker they had seen at the fun park. You could see the new tooth just starting to come out. Ellen had her arms around Jack's middle, and looked as serious as ever.

In the other photograph, they were with their mother and all of their faces were made up into horrible monster masks. His mother's eyes were wide and her mouth as well. He and Ellen were laughing wildly, but it looked as if their mother was screaming silently rather than laughing.

Ellen's words came back to him. She had said that secrets got inside their mother and made her sick.

Sick? Where had Ellen got the idea that their mother was sick? She had never been in hospital and she hardly ever went to the doctor. There were the pills, but she bought them from a chemist so there couldn't be anything that bad wrong with her. You needed a prescription for anything that was really wrong. His mother said they were to stop her from feeling unhappy, but unhappiness wasn't a sickness, was it?

Ellen might have thought being sad was the same as being sick, though. It was the sort of weird idea she got into her head, and it was even reasonable. He felt sick whenever he thought of his mother dying. He never let himself think of how she died and of his own part in it. That was something he put in a dark corner of his mind and he only looked there in his nightmares.

He shivered and turned from the pictures at the same time as the door opened.

A man and a woman came into the room. They were wearing old-fashioned clothes and were colourless.

Jack expected the woman to scream seeing him there, but she didn't appear to notice him. Then it dawned on him the couple were not only colourless but partly transparent. You could see things right through them. Maybe they were ghosts. Again, fear flickered and died in Jack.

'Have you the paper?' the man asked.

The woman opened her shopping bag and gave him a rolled-up newspaper. Then she took off her coat and hung it on a hook behind the door.

Jack dared not move because he was sure they would catch sight of him if he did. At the same time, he didn't understand how they hadn't seen him already.

The door opened again and Alice came in. She still had the bundle in her arms and she looked miserable but, unlike the man and woman, she was quite solid.

'I'm going to run away,' she told them. 'You'll

never see me anymore. I'm going to the grey tower.'

'The child is late,' the man said.

'Good children should be unseen and unheard,' the woman added repressively.

'Look at me!' Alice demanded.

Neither the man nor the woman looked at her.

'Nobody looks at bad children,' the mother said. 'Bad children are not seen or heard. Bad children are invisible.'

'I'm not bad,' Alice whispered. '*You're* bad!'

The man pressed his lips together and opened his paper. He began to read it and the woman started to set the table.

Alice saw Jack, and her mouth opened in surprise. She looked at the man and the woman, and then made a gesture for him to follow her.

'You came!' she whispered, clutching at his arm when they were standing together in the grey hall-way. It struck Jack suddenly that maybe the reason he kept bumping into Alice was because somehow she wanted it to happen. Certainly she seemed glad to see him, but she looked terrible. Her face was streaked with the marks of dried tears, her hair hung in matted clumps about her face and there was a raw-looking rash around her mouth.

'You went away and left me because I'm a bad noisy girl. But I can't help it. I don't mean to be. Sometimes I feel like my head will burst open and spill out all the colour and the noise.'

Jack was bewildered by her word and her degeneration, but he patted her shoulder awkwardly. 'I didn't mean to leave you just like that. A man scared me.'

'A man?' She looked in both directions. 'Maybe it was one of them.'

'Them?'

'They all want my bright thing.' She pressed the bundle to her chest and her eyes were wild. 'I won't let them have it, though. I need it. I can't have anything else, but I shall have this. I didn't steal it. He gave it to me so why shouldn't I keep it?'

'No one wants your bright thing,' Jack assured her gently. She seemed so ravaged and she clung to her precious bundle so pitifully that he found himself insisting he would help her take it to the grey tower. Suddenly satisfying his curiosity about the bundle seemed less important than helping her.

Her eyes widened in disbelief. 'Really? You don't want my bright thing for yourself? I thought that you wanted to take it back with you. I thought that was why you came.'

'I will help you bring it to the grey tower,' he repeated calmly. 'If that is what you want.'

'It is the only way,' she said and her eyes shone with tears. She glanced back over her shoulder at the closed door then said urgently, 'Let's go now.'

'Who are those people in there?' Jack asked. They were the first people he had seen other than Alice herself and the circus man. He couldn't count the beast or the reflection of the man he had seen in the window or the mythical creatures that had vanished from the circus cages. But the people in the living room had not been completely real either. They had been like holograms.

'They never look at me,' Alice muttered. 'They say I must be still and quiet. They want all the life to be gone out of me. That's what they really mean.'

Jack felt exasperated. If only she would answer his questions properly. But maybe she couldn't so there was no point in asking her again who the people were. Or anything else. If he wanted answers, he must go back to the laughing beast or figure things out for himself. But he couldn't just leave Alice the way she was.

She was staring at him, eyes gleaming. 'You will really come with me to the tower? Will you climb it with me?'

Her avid look made Jack uncomfortable and he shook his head. 'I'll come there but I won't climb it because I need to go back home. I want to see it,' he added hastily, because she might be offended by his refusal to climb it.

'You *want* to see it?' For a moment Alice looked wistful and her sharp little face was very pretty.

'I promised to go with you and I will,' Jack said briskly.

'We have to go back to the circus, then,' Alice said.

Her eyes seemed to grow cloudy. 'I like the circus. All those animals in the cages, pacing and pacing with their white teeth showing. I am like a caged animal in this house. I am pacing and pacing and my keepers are outside the bars watching me.' She glanced back at the closed door. 'Once I go up the grey tower I will be free of them forever.'

Alice's voice had risen and Jack feared that the people in the living room would hear her. Even ghost people gifted at not seeing might be compelled to notice him if there was enough trouble. And he did not want to see them again, he realised. There had been something ugly in the way they had ignored Alice. Something very calculated and cruel.

'Why did you come here? That bald man said there are other winged people like you at the circus,' Jack said. 'Couldn't you stay with them?'

'Not until I go to the grey tower,' Alice said dully.

'But haven't you already been there?' Jack asked. He pointed to her shrouded wings.

Alice frowned and seemed confused. 'I have been to the grey tower and I am going there always.'

'That doesn't make any sense,' Jack said gently, quietly in the hope that she would drop her voice too.

'It is this . . .' She stared down at the bundle with a kind of rage, and then she cuddled it to her. 'I have to take it to the grey tower, then we can *both* be free.' Jack experienced a sudden savage impulse to snatch the bundle out of her hands. He was shocked both by the strength of his urge, and the urge itself. Whatever was in the bundle belonged to Alice and taking it from her would be a monstrous act.

But as if he had no control over himself, Jack's eyes again fell to the bundle. He had the weird feeling that it was calling to him. Yearning for him to touch it. The desire to take it rose in him again and, horrified at himself, Jack clenched his fists. It would be like taking something from his little sister, and he would never do that, but the desire to see what was in the bundle seemed to go through him like a fever.

Alice saw his fingers twitch and when she saw his expression, her eyes widened in fear.

All at once, there was a growling sound right beside them.

'Wolver,' Alice screamed, and Jack screamed too as something leapt out of the shadows at him. He reeled back at the glass door but there was nothing there and he was falling.

'Are you in there, Jack?' Ellen called, hammering on his door.

Jack sat up in bed and looked at his clock. It said six-thirty. On a Saturday. He got up and opened the door to stare out at his sister. 'What are you doing? It's the weekend!'

'I know it is,' Ellen said. 'It's the Saturday we're going and see Grandma. Daddy said we're going in five minutes.'

Jack shut the door and dressed, repressing the urge to groan, and wondered if he wouldn't rather be fighting wolvers in the greylands.

Lacing his sneakers, he grabbed his cap and a book he was reading and came out into the hall. Ellen came out of her room with the fairy tale book and Mr Foo.

'Someone from the mall rang to say your bag was there,' his father said, coming out and putting on his jacket.

He didn't look at Jack directly, and Jack thought of the two people in the greylands who had ignored Alice. He had got the feeling they found some nasty pleasure in pretending not to see Alice, but there was no cruelty in his father. He was just . . . emptied out.

Jack was filled with pity for his father, but also with the same old helplessness. He could get out of the visit by just refusing to go. His father would not have the energy to fight him, but in fairness to Ellen he said nothing. He didn't mind visiting his grandmother, in fact, but he disliked Aunt Rose, who was not really his aunt but the old woman's long-time companion. She was a tall, cold woman with a sharp nose and a matching voice. Her eyes reminded him of the eyes of those birds that peck the worms out of their holes.

Fifteen minutes later, Jack snapped Ellen into her seat belt and himself beside her. They were both in the back seat so he could read to her. His father just got in the car like a robot and turned the key. He never said a word. They had a whole load of silence aboard. In ten minutes they were at the highway entrance. There were hardly any cars on the road because it was so early, and Jack looked out at the empty streets thinking that in this dull, hazy, early morning light, they might have been driving through the greylands.

The highway circled back over the edge of town and when they passed above the fun park with its unmistakable blue-and-white striped big top, framed by the white latticing of the roller coaster behind it, both Jack and Ellen gazed down at it. It opened weekends when it was fine, but was still closed now because it was so early. A few rays of sun had broken through the frayed edges of the clouds and lit some of the shadowy paths. Something flashed brightly, and Jack wondered if it was the mirror outside the maze.

'Read to me?' Ellen asked, when the fun park was out of sight.

'All right. But pick something short.'

'The one about the lovers that never got old,' Ellen said decisively.

'But you've heard that one before lots of times.'

'That's what I want to hear,' Ellen said.

Jack sighed and flipped through the pages until he found the story.

'Once there was a woman who came across the world to give a speech in another land,' Jack read, then faltered, for surely this was the story Alice had asked for in the greylands.

'Go on,' Ellen prompted. 'She was very tired . . .'

'She was very tired when she arrived, but she had to go to a banquet in a cellar under an old monastery. As she went down the stone steps, the ancient cold of the place fell around her like a mantle of snow. She had never been so cold in her life before. The servant bringing her there saw that she was shivering. "This is a strange place," he said. "This cold is not natural but is caused because all the four winds of the world come together in this place." The woman's skin tingled and the hair on her neck rose, for it seemed to her that anything might happen in such a place.'

'Anything can happen,' Ellen whispered to Mr Foo.

'The servant led the woman into an enormous room with a low domed roof. There were no electric lights, and the place was lit by a huge fire and candles which cast grotesque shadows, making the small group of men and women seem like a crowd of thousands all flickering and shifting and turning their pale, unknown faces to her.'

'She was lonely among all of those strange people,' Ellen said solemnly.

'She looked around the room, searching for a kind face, because she was so very tired she felt she would not be able to talk sensibly. Then across the room, she saw a man.'

'A tall man,' Ellen breathed.

'A tall, stooping man with brown eyes and a smile that lit up his face. The woman began to move towards the man, for she felt such a face could only belong to a person of great goodness.'

'The man saw her.'

'He did, and her began to move towards her. They reached one another and in the very centre of that room when they touched hands, all the power of the four winds rushed at them, and wove the air together around them.'

'They fell in love like Mama and Daddy did,' Ellen murmured softly, and Jack remembered this story had been their mother's favourite and the reason she had bought the book. She had told them this was how it had been when she and their father met.

Jack looked at his father's back but it was as steady as a stone.

'Read the rest,' Ellen ordered.

'They became blind to all of the other people in the room for it seemed to them both that everything in the world they wanted to know lay in the eyes of the other. There was no need to look anywhere else.'

They danced and the four winds plucked at their hair and whispered in their ears. The couple went from that place to the country where the man lived. There was a war, but they did not see the soldiers marching. They sat on the edge of a fountain and bullets whispered around them. They went to the woman's country and there was a festival with choirs and flowery garlands, but they did not hear the singing nor smell the flowers. They did not have to look anywhere but into one another to see and hear and smell everything. They walked by seas and over mountains until they had travelled around the whole world. They did not notice time passing, and after a while, time did not notice them. It flowed by them with the four winds. Ages passed and they walked through the streets again and again. They saw no one, but they could be seen by some people, glowing gold and bright.'

'They were ghosts?' Ellen asked.

'They never died so they couldn't be ghosts. They were a legend and their story passed from ear to ear and land to land. They walked the same streets they had walked centuries before, and they sat in the same squares and fountains, and year after year people came to watch them. They would call their friends and gather on the corners to witness the immortal lovers. No one attempted to touch them or wake them from their dream of love, for as the world grew dark with war and sadness, the lovers shone ever more brightly, and people came to them to warm their souls and renew their hope. That's the end.'

'The end,' Ellen echoed. She frowned and Jack had the feeling she had hoped it might come out differently this time. Little kids were funny that way. They didn't seem to realise a book was fixed. It was a peculiar story though, Jack thought, passing it to Ellen so she could look at the final picture of two glowing lovers walking all unaware past the crowds of wretched shadowy people. He had never noticed it before but although the lovers glowed with colour, the people watching were all black and white. It was like looking into the greylands.

Jack shivered and could not imagine why their mother had loved that sombre little story so much. Maybe it was because she and their father had met like that in some other country, and had fallen in love. Only *their* love hadn't lived forever.

His father had not spoken or glanced around once, since they had got into the car. He was like a statue.

He belongs in the greylands, Jack found himself thinking.

'So, you've come,' Aunt Rose said coldly.

Jack got out and let Ellen out and they both stared up at the tall woman. She was dressed in a shapeless beige skirt, a brown shirt and shoes.

'She's getting worse and worse,' she told their father. 'She walks and walks. I had a call yesterday at five a.m. The garbage collector said he almost hit her!'

'Maybe it's time she went in a home,' Jack's father suggested.

Something tightened in Aunt Rose's face. 'That would cost a great deal, David.'

Jack knew from other discussions between Aunt Rose and his father that Aunt Rose could only stay in the house as long as their grandmother did. After the old woman's death, she would inherit whatever remained of the estate, including the house but the only way the old woman could go into an expensive nursing home would be if the house was sold, which would leave nowhere for Aunt Rose to live, and nothing to inherit.

'You might as well come in,' she snapped ungraciously.

The house was neat and smelled faintly of disinfectant. The grey carpet was smooth and the furniture worn but of good quality. The fireplace had been boarded up and an electric heater installed. Suddenly Jack's mouth fell open, for there on the mantelpiece were the pictures he had seen in the greylands! The one of his father giving them a seesaw and his mother's silent scream. The room was different, but the pictures were definitely the ones he had seen.

'Where did those pictures come from?' he asked.

Aunt Rose stared at him disapprovingly. 'There's no need to shout at me. Your grandmother brought them with her when she moved here after your grandfather died.'

Jack was too puzzled by the mystery to make any explanations for his question. Let Aunt Rose think what she liked. He was suddenly certain that the living room he had seen in the greylands must have been the one in his grandmother's *old* house, which he could barely remember. It had been sold after his grandfather died.

'Do you have any other photographs?' he asked.

'Photographs?' Aunt Rose looked at him, as if he had asked for shrunken heads.

'Who are these children?'

They all turned to the thin, elderly woman entering from the kitchen. Her hair was white and cut short and she wore a blue dress and a matching shawl. Her eyes were narrowed and her mouth twisted to one side as if she had tasted something bad.

'Hello, Grandma,' Ellen said. She made no move to hug the old woman, who did not like to be touched.

'Children should be seen and not heard,' the old woman said. Then her face lost its animation. She said in a flat, vague whining voice, 'I can't find the teapot.'

Jack actually heard Aunt Rose grinding her teeth. 'I have shown you a thousand times. I wish you would remember.'

'This house is new to me,' the old woman said querulously. 'You expect a lot from an old woman.' Aunt Rose gave Jack's father a long-suffering look of fury and then ushered the old woman into the kitchen. Their father followed wordlessly.

'She's forgetting,' Ellen said to Jack, plumping herself down on a chair. 'All of her life is leaking out of her. Soon there will be nothing left.' She said this quite cheerfully. Then she eyed her brother. 'Why do you want to see old photographs?'

He shrugged. 'I just want to see what Grandma looked like when she was young. I want to see their old house.'

'Why?'

'Just,' Jack said impatiently.

Ellen shrugged. 'There's a picture in the hall of Grandma and the old house.'

Jack stood eagerly. 'Show me.'

Jack had walked past the old photograph a hundred times, but he had never really looked at it. The woman in it, standing in a garden, was the woman from Alice's house in the greylands, the woman who had handed the man a paper. But it was impossible to tell if the house behind her in the photograph was the same as the one he had seen in the Greylands.

'What's the matter?' Ellen asked. 'You've gone all white.'

Jack wondered what she would say if he told her he had seen their grandmother as a young woman in the greylands. But how had she come to be there? Was it because of her grandmother forgetting things that she had gone there? The first time he had entered the greylands, Alice had told him you could only get there if you were wounded. Maybe forgetting was a kind of wounding. Memories leaking out could constitute a bleeding, couldn't they? Did she go to and fro like Jack had done, without even knowing it? Or was it that memories were a kind of reflection. Maybe the house in the greylands and his grandfather were just his grandmothers' memories.

'Grandmother, what was your old house like?' he asked, when they were all in the living room.

Aunt Rose looked at Jack suspiciously, but she could find nothing to criticise, so she pursed her lips disagreeably.

'My house?' the old woman sniffed. 'That was the one before this. I lived there . . . a long time ago. With Arthur. He didn't like noise and talk and neither did I. There were roses, but we didn't cut them down because they were the kind that didn't smell and there were no thorns.'

'I like roses that smell,' Ellen said.

'Children should be seen and not heard,' the old woman hissed. 'Children should not smell or have thorns.'

Aunt Rose sighed loudly. 'You see what I have to put up with, David. You should hear how she talks to the neighbour's children. How on earth she let herself have a child is beyond me when she dislikes them so. No wonder your poor wife . . .' She stopped.

Jack was thinking about how it must have been for his mother to have lived with his grandmother, who hated children and the smell of roses, and his grandfather, who wanted only silence and order. Like

Alice she must have felt like a caged animal pacing backwards and forwards.

Jack almost gasped aloud as an incredible thought occurred to him.

Could it possibly be that Alice in the greylands was his mother as a little girl?

With a terrible chill, Jack understood suddenly why Alice was attracted to the circus.

On this side of the mirror it was the fun park where his mother had died.

Chapter 11

'Do you really feel sick?' Ellen asked him doubtfully.

Jack nodded because it was true. He was sick with fear.

'Aunt Rose was mad that we didn't stay for dinner,' Ellen said.

Jack said nothing and neither did their father. He had not seemed to care when Jack had announced suddenly that he was ill, and wanted to go home. He had simply risen and said they would go. He didn't answer any of Aunt Rose's indignant protests and, as they were going out the door, she had given him a puzzled look.

Jack took Ellen's hand and squeezed it, to comfort both her and himself.

'Your hand is cold,' she said.

Jack didn't know what to say. He looked out the window and pretended to be watching the houses they passed. He just couldn't make casual conversation when every bone in his body was screaming at him to hurry. He prayed his father's dull unquestioning manner would hold out because his plan was very flimsy.

He made up his mind that if it failed, he would say he had to throw up and, when the car stopped, he would open the door and run.

As they came over the bridge at last, he said casually but firmly that he felt carsick and could they stop so he could get some fresh air.

'We can't stop on the bridge,' his father said.

Jack had expected that, and asked in as calm a voice as he could manage if they might turn off after the bridge then because he felt really terrible. The first road after the bridge led to the beach and at the other end of the beach was the fun park.

'Let's stop at the beach, Daddy,' Ellen said. 'We can go for a walk.'

Jack feared that his father would remember that the fun park was up the other end of the beach. He might be numb, but he could not be so numb that he had forgotten the place where his wife had died.

Jack's mind twitched nervously to the story about the immortal lovers as they approached the end of the bridge. He was imagining what would have happened if someone had managed to get the attention of one of the lovers. The magic was in their never looking away from each another, so if one of them had broken that endless looking, would they both have been pulled back into time, or just the one distracted? And if one were left, wouldn't he be like

Jack's father? A grey ghost drifting hopelessly, never smiling or speaking unless he must. Never caring for anything again? Unable to laugh?

The blinker clicked and the car swung smoothly off the main road after they left the bridge. The sea glittered ahead, at the end of the street they had entered and Jack had a flickering memory of sitting on the beach watching his mother swim across the waves. There were a few other cars and some people near the car park throwing a Frisbee for a silky black Labrador.

'I wish we had a dog,' Ellen sighed as Jack got out.

'I'm just going to walk a bit,' Jack said quickly.

'Can I come?' Ellen asked.

'No!' he said, too sharply.

Her face fell.

'It . . . it's just that I don't want you watching me throw up,' Jack added quickly.

Ellen's face cleared. 'Okay. Maybe we can go for a walk after you throw up.'

'Sure,' Jack said. 'Uh. I'll be back soon, Dad.'

Again his father made no response, but Jack was in too much of a hurry to care that he had hardly said a word the whole day. As soon as he was out of sight of the car, he broke into a run and, unlike in the greylands, the ground flew under him.

His heart was pounding as his fear for Alice mounted. He remembered that his mother had talked of flying the day she died, and Alice too had mentioned flying once she reached the grey tower.

At last he reached the start of the boardwalk. He looked back. It was about a kilometre from the car park and another kilometre along it lay the fun park, so even if Ellen realised something was amiss and managed to rouse their father, it would take them some time to come after him.

A guy with a bald, tattooed head rollerbladed to a sudden stop right in front of Jack, pivoted and headed back the other way. An old man and lady were strolling arm in arm a little further along the boardwalk, and the old man shook his fist at the bald guy as he roared past. There was no one else on the boardwalk until it got closer to the fun park, and from the crowd there, it was clearly open.

Jack ran past the elderly couple and tried to match the rollerblader in speed. When it was too congested to run, he left the boardwalk and ran over the warm sand.

At last he came to the huge grinning smile that was the entrance to the park. There was a long line of people waiting to buy a ticket to get in and Jack took his place, gritting his teeth at the delay.

'Need to go to the toilet, do you?' a plump, freckle-faced older girl behind him asked with a grin, and Jack realised he had been jiggling up and down in his impatience. He would have been embarrassed if he hadn't been so scared. He didn't know what she saw in his face, but her grin faded.

Jack turned back to the front, willing the line to move faster.

At last his turn came, but as he reached into his pocket, he was horrified to discover he had left his wallet with his cap and book in the car.

'You want to step aside?' the ticket seller said around the end of a black stub of cigar. 'No freebies.'

Jack stared at him desperately, wondering if he dared to run and try to lose himself in the crowds. A hand reached past him and slapped down the entrance fee, and he turned to see the freckle-faced girl.

'On me, kid,' she said, and handed him the ticket. 'Hotfoot it.'

'Thanks,' he said fervently, and ran through the mouth into the park. He tore along the alley leading to the sideshows, pushing, and weaving through the milling weekend crowds until he came to the mirror maze. There was a mirror outside, there was no way he could go through it into the greylands with all these people watching. He would have to go inside the maze. Fortunately the entrance ticket entitled him to one free ride.

'Step in,' a man called from the booth outside the door of the mirror maze. 'See yourself as you've never seen yourself. See what it would be like to have eyes in the back of your head!'

Jack stumbled up to the booth.

'Hey!' a woman said indignantly. 'Wait your turn.'

He turned and saw that there was a long line snaking to the side of the booth.

'Back of the line,' the doorman said, waving him away.

Biting his lip, Jack retreated. He had the feeling every second counted, and he was terribly afraid he knew now what the grey tower was. He noticed the flap to the Monster Man's tent alongside the mirror maze was partly open, though there was no one selling tickets at the box. He slipped inside hoping there would be a way to get from it into the mirror maze.

Unexpectedly, the tent did not have a short entrance tunnel like the others. The flap opened straight into the main part of the tent, which was smaller than it looked from the outside. There were several rows of empty seats facing a booth. There was a spotlight above the booth, but it was switched off. Nonetheless, Jack could see that there was someone sitting in the alcove.

'Hello,' a soft voice greeted him.

Jack went closer and saw that there was a man sitting on his haunches in the alcove. In the dull light he looked nearly colourless enough to have been in the greylands. His face was twisted and his nose and mouth were grotesquely big while his eyes were too small and of two different colours.

'The tent was open,' Jack said quickly.

'Oh yes. It's open all right, but not many people

come in here to look at me now so there's no point in selling tickets. No one is interested in a man who professes to be a monster. They'll give me notice very soon. I started out being a great attraction, but people soon understood that what fascinated them about me was no more than the reflections of their own deformities. All I do is show them what is inside themselves,' he added mournfully.

'You don't look like a monster to me,' Jack said. Distracted by the plight of the big ugly man. 'Maybe you could get another sort of job.'

'Oh, I *am* a monster!' the man said earnestly. 'Really. If you could see inside me you would know the truth. I am not like these other people with monsters inside and handsome faces on the outside. I am monster through and through. There's nothing a monster can do but be a monster.'

'Maybe it's you who doesn't see the truth of yourself,' Jack said. 'Maybe inside you is not a monster but someone handsome and good.' He looked around. 'Can you tell me if there is a way into the maze of mirrors next door from your tent?'

The man was staring at him with a strange expression. Then he started. 'Oh, I . . . forgive me. There is a way but it is forbidden for customers.'

'Please,' Jack begged. 'It's a matter of life and death.'

The man nodded. 'I can see that. And you have been kind to spend a few moments with me though

I can see you are in a rush. You have given me
something to think about in saying I might not be a
monster inside. I had never thought of that . . .' He
pointed away from the alcove to the side of the tent.
'Behind the curtain there are panels. One of them
will swing open and let you through. But you won't
be able to come back that way. It only works the one
way.'

'Thank you,' Jack said fervently. He started towards the curtain, and then he stopped and reached
into his pocket. He took out the long feather Alice
had lost when her wing was trapped and went back
to give it to the man.

His ugly face lit up. 'Really? A gift for me?' He took
the feather reverently and stroked his cheek with it.
He closed his eyes in ecstasy. 'So soft. So beautiful.'
To Jack's astonishment the feather blushed scarlet,
and the tip shimmered with gold. The man laughed
in excitement, and his eyes glowed.

'You should laugh when you look in the mirror,'
Jack blurted out, thinking that if he could not give
the laughing beast a gift, at least he would uncage as
much laughter as he could.

'Many people have laughed at me in my life, but
I have never laughed at myself . . .' the man said.
The feather threw a golden light into his mismatched
eyes.

'I have to go,' Jack said, and he hurried to the canvas and wriggled through a slit in it. Behind it were

panels and he pushed at them until one swung open.

He stepped into the mirror maze and the panel behind him clicked decisively. He was in a straight tunnel lined with mirrors and turning away at both ends to yet more mirrors. Thousands of Jacks looked one way and then the other in the dim lighting, trying to decide which way to go. Somewhere he heard a girl laughing. She sounded on the edge of hysteria.

'Don't!' a child shrieked, from another direction.

'That has to be the way out . . .' a man said.

'It's a trick . . .'

Jack whirled to face whoever had whispered into his ear, but he was alone in this part of the maze. Belatedly he realised it had sounded like his mother's voice.

'She's afraid of mirrors . . .' Ellen had said.

'If she is afraid of mirrors she is afraid of herself,' the laughing beast had said.

Jack stopped his ears to the voices and concentrated because somehow he had to get through a mirror into the greylands. He chose one of the mirrors and stared at it, but he was distracted by his eyes staring at him from a hundred other mirrors and angles.

Then he heard a shout that sounded like Alice's voice.

'Alice?' he called.

'Alice Alice Alice . . . A faint echo mocked him, sounding now like his mother.

He shivered and so did his mirror image. The

shivering continued when he had stopped and Jack reached out to let the mirror draw him into itself. The sound of a baby crying, the carnival music, the laughter and the hum of voices simply switched off.

Jack stepped into another hall of mirrors exactly the same as the other, except that he was very pale and the tent roof had changed from green to black.

'Alice?' he called into the flat silence.

'Alice . . . Ali . . . lissa . . . Lissa . . .'

Jack shuddered because Lissa was his mother's real name.

'Mama?' he whispered, because he was calling up a ghost.

Somewhere far away he heard the howling of the wolvers and the skin on his arms rose up in goose-bumps. The air felt neither hot nor cold, and yet Jack was chilled to the bone. He thought of the woman in the story stepping into the ancient crypt where the four winds met, and wondered if the man and woman had loved each other, or had simply been joined together by some accident of powers converging on them.

He saw a movement in one of the mirrors and recognised Alice.

'Hey!' he cried. 'Wait!'

'Shhh,' she whispered, and her face looked out from behind him. He whirled and so did his own reflections. Again he was at the centre of a thousand eyes, all his own.

'Where are you?' Jack shouted, growing angry because he was scared. 'Come out Alice. I have to talk to you.'

Another flicker and Jack was stunned to see his mother darting across the mirrors.

'Mama!' he cried. 'Mama, wait. Alice. Lissa . . .' He ran along the mirrored corridor in the direction she had gone, and came to a fork.

He stopped, remembering that this was how it had happened the day she died.

She had brought them to the fun park for a birthday treat. They had ridden over the white-painted grid of struts holding up the curves of the roller-coaster circuit and on the ghost train and they had eaten fairy-floss, and last of all they had gone into the maze, leaving Ellen in the blow-up castle with a friend she had met.

'You don't like mirrors,' Jack said.

'They lie,' his mother said. 'But they show the truth too. I must face the truth now.'

Jack did not know what she meant, but he did not like the way the bones of her face seemed to press out against the skin as if something in there was fighting to be free.

'Let's go on the Ferris wheel instead,' he said, tugging at her.

'The mirrors must be faced,' she only said grimly, and paid the ticket seller.

'One adult and one halfling,' he said, baring a gapped grin. 'See yourself, beautiful lady, and see if you can find the way out. Enter the maze of mirrors and you will see yourself as you have never been seen. Only after you have faced your deepest self, in the test of the mirrors, will you be free!'

They went into the maze. The first corridor of mirrors led to a fork. 'You go one way and I will go the other,' his mother said. 'Everyone must travel their own path and find their own way home. That is the rule.'

Jack did not want to be separated because he found the myriad reflections of himself and his mother frightening. But it was his birthday and he did not want to seem a baby. So they parted.

He took the left way and, ignoring the faces, doggedly turned left and left and left every time. That was how he solved paper mazes. He came to several dead-ends and had to turn back. Twice he passed the thick cement power pole around which the maze had been constructed before he finally found his way out.

'Home free,' the booth man said, giving him a shining star to wear. 'But where is the beautiful lady?'

'She must be lost in there.' Jack had been elated to think that he had found his way out first, but after a few more minutes he began to get worried. He was remembering how much his mother hated mirrors, and how strangely she had acted going into the maze. He asked the man if he could go in and find her.

The man began to refuse, but something in Jack's face seemed to change his mind. He went in himself but a few moments later he came out shaking his head. 'She's not in there.'

'But she must be. She went in and she didn't come out. Unless there is an other way out?'

The man shook his head. 'The maze goes to the ground so people can't cheat. And there would be no way to climb out of it except . . .' He paled and ran out into the centre of the path to look up.

Chapter 12

Jack could not bear to go on remembering what had happened next. He turned his mind to Alice. The wolvers howled and snarled, sounding much closer than before but his fear of them was nothing to his fear for Alice.

'Hey!' he cried, and he began to penetrate the maze, searching for the power pole his mother had climbed that terrible day. 'Alice!'

'Alice . . . Aliss . . . Lissa . . .' The echoes ran on for too long.

The maze was much more complex in the grey-lands. He would never find the pole unless he went into the real world. He looked into a mirror and deliberately thought of Ellen. The mirror sucked him back into the real world. Laughter and music and voices swirled around him. He could smell hot dogs and fairy-floss and chips as he began to try in earnest to solve the maze and find his way to the centre.

He ran for a bit, pushing the mirrors because he remembered from before that there were mirrors within the maze that were doors which would bring you more quickly to the centre, if you could find them.

A mirror creaked as he touched it and he stepped through into the next tunnel. He thought he saw his mother and ran, only to be sucked through another mirror. The sound ceased and he was back in the greylands. Suddenly he understood. The thought of Ellen would bring him into the real world, but the thought of his mother brought him into the greylands. He had been thinking about his mother the night he first entered the greylands.

He heard Alice's voice and realised she was reflected all around him. A thousand Alices. An infinity of Alices pressing ragged bundles to their chests. Even now, he wondered what was in the bundle.

'Are you coming?' she asked.

'There is something I need to tell you,' Jack said urgently, stepping towards her. 'You mustn't go up the grey tower, Alice. You'll fall if you do. You'll be killed.'

She laughed and shrugged to make the cloak fall off her shoulders. Her wings fluttered. 'I cannot fall.'

'I have never seen you fly,' Jack pointed out urgently. 'Never.'

A shadow passed over her face. 'Those with wings can fly,' she said. But it was not an answer.

'Have you ever flown?' Jack took another step towards her thinking that if he could just get close enough he could grab her.

'I will fly when I have climbed the grey tower. When my shining thing can fly with me. If you come with us, you will have wings to fly. Come, Jack. Come with us. It will be so wonderful. We can fly up out of the grey-lands and into the sky. There will be the four winds singing and all the lost colours of the rainbow.'

Her face blazed with beauty and Jack could not speak.

'Come, Jack,' she whispered, and then she darted sideways.

Jack gathered his wits and plunged after her, but almost at once he came to a dead-end. Panicking, he turned and the wolvers howled. He froze, for they sounded as if they were on the other side of the mirrors. But he must find Alice. That was more important than being afraid of the wolvers. He must save her as he had failed to save his mother. He must.

He ran.

When he finally reached the power pole, he found a long silky feather at the bottom.

He looked up through the gap between the canvas roof of the mirror maze, and the pole soaring up and above the fun park.

He heard someone crying. His mother or Alice, he no longer knew which was which, and perhaps they were the same. It didn't matter. To save one would be to save the other, as he had failed to do before. His mother had fallen to her death with a terrified scream that he still heard falling and falling through his dreams. Then she had lain like a broken bird, blood leaking from her ears, the light from the hole she had torn in the tent making her pale face shine. He had cried out her name, but she had looked up and her eyes had been full of the sky and the clouds.

'Alice!' he called up the power pole.

She did not answer, and so he began to climb the iron rods sticking out from the cement pole. He squeezed through the gap between the tent and the pole.

'Alice!' He stared up but the sun was in his eyes. Nevertheless he saw a flash of white he knew must be wings.

He climbed, careful not to look down. 'Alice!'

'Come . . .' her voice floated down to him.

He climbed higher and higher until at last he reached the small platform where she was sitting. She helped him up onto it, and below them the circus and the plain and the city seemed to be a flat board, so high had they risen.

'You see,' Alice said, her eyes wild with excitement. She still had the bundle in her arms. 'We are almost in the sky.'

'Please come down with me,' Jack pleaded. 'You have never tried your wings and you don't know if they will carry you. Practise flying first.'

'There is no time,' Alice said with calm certainly, and she began to unwrap the bundle.

Jack stared, mesmerised as the folds were peeled back.

'What is it?' he whispered, for though it was unwrapped, it was so bright he could not look at it. Oddly, he seemed to hear laughter, faint and beautiful as a song.

Alice shuddered as if the laughter cut her but she rose with the shining thing she had taken from the bundle and Jack realised with horror that she meant to throw it down.

A terrible fear smote him, though he did not know why. 'Don't . . .' he whispered weakly, his fear so great it had stolen all of his strength.

'It belongs to me. It was a gift,' Alice said defensively, and behind the radiance she was suddenly his mother, her long dark hair waving in skeins like smoke. 'He gave it to me.'

'He?' Jack's lips felt numb. The laughter from the bright thing shimmered and seemed to make the air golden.

'He. The immortal lover. He gave me his soul and his heart. He gave me himself. He belongs to me.'

Jack began to shiver violently, for at last he understood and he was more afraid than he had ever been in his life. His father could not laugh anymore because his soul was in the greylands where laughter was caged. *That* was what the bright thing was.

'Please,' he whispered. 'He loved you. Don't take him with you.'

'He wants to come. He dwells already in the grey-lands because I am lost to him. I will bring him to me. We belong together forever. It must be so.'

'What about me and Ellen, Mama? Will you bring us all into the greylands?'

Confusion passed over a face that was both his mother's and Alice's. The bright thing that was his father's spirit, radiant in her hands, rained light on them.

'Children should not be seen. They should not . . .' She faltered.

'That's not true,' Jack cried against a rising wind. 'That was your mother and father and they were wrong. Children *have* to be heard. How else can they tell you they love you?'

'Stop saying these things to me,' Alice snarled. 'I won't listen. I want him and he belongs to me.'

'He loves us,' Jack cried. 'He is alive and so are we. He belongs with us now.'

It was the wrong thing to say he knew it as soon as he said it. Alice was beyond reason. She was sick with sadness and she had swallowed up secrets and most of what had been his mother with her fears and her longing to fly. His mother had died and Alice was all that was left of her.

The wolvers gave their freezing howls and Jack seemed to hear the anguished laughter of the beast as his mother slowly raised the bright thing high above her head.

She swayed in the wind.

'Mama, don't take him. We need him,' Jack whispered. 'Please. He will not forget you if you let him stay with us. He will love you forever and every time he laughs, he will remember how you once laughed . . .'

Tears were running down his cheeks, but he did not care if he looked like a baby.

Slowly, so slowly, she lowered her arms. Holding the shining thing to her, she leaned down and reached one hand to touch his cheek, and again she was his mother. Her eyes were dry and so sad. 'My son,' she whispered. 'My darling Jack.'

'I love you, Mama,' Jack said.

She pressed the bundle of rags and the gleaming brightness it contained into his arms.

'Goodbye, Jack. Tell him . . . tell him I will love him forever . . .'

She stood up and swayed back. Jack screamed as he realised what she was doing, but even as he reached desperately for her, she fell away from his hands. She was his mother, not Alice, and there were no wings to carry her up to the clouds. There was only falling and falling and then the sound of tearing, and of shattered mirrors.

Jack pressed his face into the pole and wept.

'Jack!'

Jack shivered at the thought that the wind had

learned his name. He did not know how long he had been hugging the grey pole, but he was stiff with cold. The ground and the fun park were far below, and all the four winds raged in the air around him.

'Jack!'

This time he opened his eyes, for it could not be the wind that sounded so frightened.

He looked down, and saw his father coming up towards him. Had he come back into the real world, or was his father finally in the greylands?

'Jack, don't move. I'm coming to get you.'

'It's my fault she died. I should have saved her,' Jack wept. The wind froze the tears on his cheeks to hard little pellets of ice.

'It was not your fault. It was never your fault. She was ill for a long time . . .'

His father was now level with him. 'Come, put your arms around my neck.'

'I didn't save her. I should have stopped her from climbing the grey tower.'

'She had been climbing the grey tower all her life, son,' his father said. 'Put your arms around me. Please.'

Jack stared into his father's lined face, and thought how tired he looked, and how afraid. Dimly it occurred to him that his father feared for him. He thought he could hear the wolvers and he wished he had fallen with his mother rather than have to tell his father again that he had failed to save her.

'She left you because she loved you . . .' he said.

His father flinched as if someone had struck him. But he did not take his eyes away from Jack's eyes. 'She loved me as much as she could, but it was hard for her. She had not been loved as a child and she had to learn to love me and to trust my love. But in the end all the sadness of not being loved when she was little made her sick. She climbed the grey tower to get away from the sadness.'

'She went into the greylands,' Jack said. 'You went after her.'

Jack's father nodded, his dark eyes deep and full of sorrow. 'I loved her and I could not see how to live without her. I . . . I left you and Ellen. I was there with you but my spirit had gone with her . . .'

'She took it with her because she loved you,' Jack said. 'She couldn't bear to leave you because she thought you would forget her.'

'I was afraid to remember her because it hurt me too much. Jack, put your arms around me and let's go down. Ellen will be frightened.'

Jack glanced down, thinking how many times Ellen had drawn him back safely from the greylands.

He reached out for his father and as he did so, he realised the bundle of rags clutched in his arms was empty. For a moment he was frightened, but as his father gathered him into an embrace so tight Jack thought he would be squashed, he gave a sobbing laugh, and Jack understood that Alice's bright thing

had gone back to where it belonged. It was inside his
father and it shone out of his eyes.

'I love you, Jack,' his father whispered against his
cheek. 'I'm sorry.'

And they climbed down to the smells and noise
and laughter of the real world, where they belonged,
and where Ellen waited.

The End

'Well?' Jack asked, for Ellen looked troubled.

'Daddy's spirit was in the bundle?'

'The bit of him that could laugh and play was in the bundle. The brightness of him.'

'And Alice was really Mama?'

'She was the hurt, sad part of Mama,' Jack said. 'She was the little girl who was not loved enough by her mother and father. That part was inside her always, even when she grew up. Then one day she got sick, and it grew bigger and bigger until it swallowed up the rest of her.'

'So she went to the greylands? But the greylands isn't real, is it? It's like the wolvers were really fears, right?'

'I think there is a greylands inside everyone where you go when you get sad or scared. Remember after Mama died how at first you didn't want to play with your friends or eat ice-creams and you didn't sing or laugh?'

'I was too sad.'

'So you went into the greylands.'

'But you can get out of the greylands, right?'

'You can get out if you think of laughing or loving or being loved. But sometimes maybe you need someone to remind you that you can get out.'

'You went there and you came back.'

'Because I had you and thinking of you reminded me it wasn't all greylands.'

'That's what the story means, doesn't it? That you can get back from the greylands if you love someone and they love you?'

'That's one of the things I meant, but stories are like mirrors. When you look in them you see yourself. It turns into your story, no matter who wrote it. And there's lots of stories in every story.'

'Like Mama's story about the lovers that time forgot about?'

Jack nodded. 'When she read that story, she saw herself and Dad. For her it was a story of loving forever.'

'Did Mama fall by accident or did she *want* to fall like Mrs MacKenzie says?'

'I don't think she wanted to fall. I think she climbed up to get away from the mirrors because they kept showing her Alice and the greylands. She wanted to get away from the greylands but it was like a cancer inside her. It had been growing since she was a little girl like you, and it was all through her. So she climbed too high, and she fell.'

'It wasn't your fault,' Ellen said.

'It wasn't anybody's fault. It was an accident, but it took me a long time to see that.'

'The wolvers chased her up there. She was scared of being crunched up by them.'

'She was scared because she didn't believe in herself,' Jack said. 'She couldn't believe anyone could love her because no one loved her enough when she was a little girl.'

'Daddy loved her and we loved her. Mario loved her, too.'

'We all did, but she had got used to not being loved when she was little. She couldn't believe in our loving her enough. For a long time she could, but then the sadness started growing. It made her into Alice.'

'You wouldn't have jumped, would you? In the story she wanted you to jump,' Ellen asked.

'I couldn't go because I had you to bring me back.'

'You thought of me and then you could come back,' Ellen said, then she nodded and smiled her rare, sweet smile. 'I'm glad you gave the feather to the Monster Man. It was almost the same as giving a present to the laughing beast, wasn't it?'

Jack nodded and Ellen fell silent for a moment. Then she said, 'Once upon a time there was a boy and a girl who loved one another very much. Read me that story, Jack.'

'Again?'